THE BARN

THE BARN

A DEBORAH STRONG MYSTERY

SHARON L. DEAN

Encircle Publications, LLC
Farmington, Maine U.S.A.

The Barn © 2020 Sharon L. Dean

Paperback ISBN 13: 978-1-64599-087-1
E-book ISBN 13:978-1-64599-088-8
Kindle ISBN 13: 978-1-64599-089-5

Library of Congress Control Number: 2020941320

Editor: Cynthia Brackett-Vincent
Book design: Eddie Vincent
Cover design: Christopher Wait, High Pines Creative, Inc.
Cover photographs © Getty Images

Published by: Encircle Publications, LLC
PO Box 187
Farmington, ME 04938
Visit: http://encirclepub.com
Sign up for Encircle Publications newsletter and specials
http://eepurl.com/cs8taP

For Ron

THE BARN
1991

THEY CYCLED PAST dew-coated corn stalks empty of their last harvest and orchards where apples hung ripe for picking. The two girls had forced themselves out of bed on a Saturday morning to seize the last of the warm weather before September turned into the frosts of late October, and they exchanged bicycle clothes for warm jackets and hiking boots.

Their fifty-mile route took them away from the fields and orchards and past Lake Shelby, its town beach deserted and the summer camp that took up half of the lake's shore closed for the season. The road curved and climbed, bordered by maples and oaks showing their first hint of oranges and reds. It would soon be trafficked with leaf-peepers on scenic drives along the backroads of New Hampshire.

By noon, their backs were damp with sweat and their legs burned. They descended a last hill back toward town, then turned right onto a dirt road that led to the Thompson barn. It loomed in front of them, its red paint cracking, an oversized black and white wooden cow's head poking out of the upper loft. The barn drew a certain class of Shelby's teenagers while the cow they all called Cowpie looked down, rotting from above. Couples went inside

1

to grope each other in hay they carried up to the loft. Boys went in threes or fours to drink vodka they drained from their parents' bottles, replacing it with water. Some used the barn as a place to smoke pot or get high on mushrooms. The cow looked down on all who entered the barn, watching and judging like the billboard eyes of Dr. T. J. Eckleburg in *The Great Gatsby*.

The two girls approached the barn. They rested their bikes against a lone one they found leaning against the clapboards. Surprised at the bike they recognized, they locked their right hands on the iron handle to open the long barn door. It creaked on its rollers, letting sunlight seep into the space that had been empty of farm animals for years. The smell of rotting hay permeated the air.

A barn swallow flew from the loft and perched on the rusted edge of a wheelbarrow. Beside it, a boy lay face down on a dirt floor strewn with pieces of hay. They recognized his long body, his blond hair curling just above his T-shirt. Joseph Wheeler, who would graduate with them in the spring. Shelby, New Hampshire Cooperative High School, class of 1991. He had everything. Charisma, athleticism, intelligence enough that he'd be valedictorian or salutatorian. Everything except a father, who'd been killed in Vietnam. They tiptoed closer, signaling each other to surprise him. The taller girl bent and caressed his neck. When he didn't move she knelt to shake him. When he still didn't wake, the smaller girl knelt beside her. Together, they rolled him over. His blue eyes stared at them with the unblinking gaze of the dead.

1

NEARLY THIRTY YEARS later, I recognized her instantly. Rachel Cummings. I jumped from my chair, gasping out "Rachel."

We hugged, and I could feel her pull back, the way she had shut me out the year we found Joseph Wheeler on the floor of the barn.

After the murder—for murder it was—the closeness went out of our friendship, and I knew she was holding something back. By spring, Joseph's murder had gone into the cold case files. We lost our innocence that year, and we lost each other.

I took hold of Rachel's hands and studied her face. The same dark eyes, the same high cheekbones, lips painted with that same shade of red. She still looked like Cleopatra. Blunt cut hair, black and untouched by the gray that had invaded my own, bangs brushing the top of her eyebrows. Despite her thick parka, I could see that she was still as thin as a painting done by some ancient Egyptian before the development of perspective. Time had deepened her beauty. I felt provincial next to her.

She surveyed the cubicle that served as my pitiful office space in the library and traced the nameplate on my desk. "Deborah Strong." When she said my name, her voice had the same low tone as in high school, a voice that sounded as if it were keeping secrets.

"Rachel Cummings. A friend I thought I'd never see again."

"I had to come. Where can we talk?"

I led her out of my cubicle to two chairs nestled at the side of the stacks. They weren't upholstered like the chairs in bigger libraries, but they had padded seats and a view of the church that was the library's neighbor. It was Friday, a frigid cold January morning, so there were few patrons to interrupt us. She took off her parka and fingered a scarf she wore tied against a tight-fitting white sweater. The scarf looked like silk, hand-dyed in tones of blue. Her jeans were smooth and navy with a slim fit that accented her long legs, legs that could outrun even the boys when we were in junior high.

"Why now?"

"I came for Mary's funeral."

I wanted to ask why she'd never visited when Joseph's mother was alive. Mary Wheeler had been like a mother to Rachel and her brother Teddy after their own mother died.

Jody, the library aid, rolled a book cart between two of the shelves, its wheels sounding like roller skates on the wood floor, reminding me of all the Saturdays in junior high that Rachel and I went to the roller rink in Nashua.

"Is that the only reason you're here?"

"Not exactly. When Teddy called me about Mary, I knew it was time to come back. Now that she's gone, I want to exorcise the ghosts of the past. Tell me you'll help search for who killed Joseph."

I gestured toward Jody who was more interested in our conversation than in shelving books. I turned my back and spoke low enough that she wouldn't hear us. "What could we possibly find after all these years?"

"I remember the police had said that something round and small hit his temple. Whatever that was killed him before he fell against the wheelbarrow. My dreams are filled with round objects. Someone might still have it. They have more advanced DNA testing now. We owe it to his mother to look."

I lifted a finger to tell Rachel not to move, and went over to Jody who should have been finished shelving. "You can get to these later. There are a lot of children's books to carry upstairs."

"I wish we had an elevator."

"You'll be fine. Make two trips. The kids will appreciate having more books to choose from." *And I'd appreciate having you out of earshot.* Jody wheeled the cart away, muttering something under her breath.

I went back to Rachel. "So after almost thirty years of no contact, you decide to come now when Mary's dead? You sent me a card from Paris. Were you studying art, or running from your ghosts?"

"I wasn't like you. When Joseph died, instead of needing to stay, I needed to leave. I'm finished running now. Or *trying* to be finished."

I had been finished with Joseph's death for some time and didn't want to open myself up to that pain again. "What good will it do to look for a murderer the police couldn't find thirty years ago?"

"How can you have forgotten the past?"

"I haven't *forgotten*, but losing my husband and child made my memory of Joseph fade."

"Teddy told me. I'm sorry."

"I gave up hoping you'd come back a long time ago. Why didn't you ever answer my letters?"

"It hurt too much. Whenever I thought of you, I remembered Joseph. That barn and the cow's head have haunted me ever since…"

"Ever since you left and went to that college in Savannah?"

"Worse the last year or so. Now Joseph keeps appearing in my paintings. I dream of him. Even if we can't find his killer, the search might make the images go away."

"I used to dream about him. Now I only dream of Nathan and Cathy."

"Cathy. My middle name."

"I named her after you. Catherine Rachel Strong."

"Tell me about her."

"Wait one minute." I went into my cubicle and picked up the photo I looked at every day: Nathan tanned and smiling in front of my parents' house, Cathy perched on his shoulders. It was her third birthday and we were celebrating. Beside them on the ground was a tricycle decorated with birthday ribbons. I came back and handed the photo to Rachel. "She was only three when she and Nathan died. A car plowed into them on that curvy road along the Rye coast."

"The road with all the mansions?"

"Yes. It was a beautiful Saturday. July seventeenth. I was working on a paper for a graduate class I was taking at UNH. I still remember it. The children in Henry James's *The Turn of the Screw*. Nathan took Cathy for an ice cream. Just a little dish, he said when I told him she was too young. She had so much energy. The only way we could keep her quiet was to take her for a car ride."

When Rachel looked at me, I saw her dark eyes fill, her mouth quiver. "We've had too much sorrow in our lives."

Outside, nuthatches and chickadees fed at a seed cone that hung from a tree at the side of the church next door. Whenever I watched them, I thought of Cathy, who was just learning the names of birds when she died. "When they died, I had to leave Portsmouth. I couldn't drive the Rye Beach road where it happened and not break down. So I came home. Lived with my parents."

"You still live with them?"

"No. I bought my own house."

"And became a librarian in a tiny town. Population what? Fifteen hundred?"

"We've grown. Pushing three thousand now."

The library door opened and a mother with two preschoolers

came inside as they always did on Friday mornings. Their routine filled a gap in my heart. "It feels like home. The library's my sanctuary."

"How were you able to heal enough to find it?"

"Our minister helped me through the darkest days. You remember him. Charles Tibbetts."

"Teddy told me you're involved with the church. I'm surprised."

I understood Rachel's surprise. We both had been doubters in high school. I tried to explain what I hardly understood myself. "Christianity doesn't require believing in some anthropomorphic God or a virgin birth. It's metaphor. And mystery."

"So you're still an atheist?"

"I'm not sure I ever was. I think it was rebellion against that Sunday school teacher we had in elementary school. She asked if we could see the face of Jesus in some painting. Everyone could except me."

"I lied. I couldn't see Jesus either. And you couldn't see to the next pew without your glasses. Contacts or laser surgery?"

"Contacts. I've been wearing them ever since college."

"So what does the church provide you now?"

"Community. I was in pain and it took me in. It gave me the strength to keep on living even though it doesn't explain suffering. There's beauty in religion. Think of all the art and the music it's produced." I parroted a cliché that didn't explain why I had returned to what I thought of as the church more than a religion.

"And the wars."

"I weighed the scales: Is the church a stronger force for good or for evil? I chose the good."

"So to do this, you came back to Shelby and chose the life of a small town librarian. You were an English major, right? Do you even have a degree in library science? As I remember, our little library in the town hall had no real librarian, just that Bertha person. I'm sure she never went to college."

"Bertha Whetmore. She's still alive, comes to the library every Tuesday. I suppose I'm like her, finding refuge among the books." I fell back into my high school role. Defending myself to this woman who was once my friend, and who had a stronger personality than my own.

"You're not at all like her!" Rachel was giving me confidence the way she used to. "She was a shriveled old lady even when we were in high school. You, on the other hand, look great."

I appreciated the compliment. I wasn't glamorous like Rachel, but I took care not to look like a spinster librarian. My clothes were all sporty, and my body as trim as it was in high school. I was a librarian who spent as much time exercising outside as reading books inside.

"We just thought she was shriveled because we were young," I said. Bertha was shriveled now and often confused. But proud. She sat in the same spot every Tuesday. "Sometimes when she's here, she thinks she's in the old library in the town hall. We've come a long way since then. I went to Simmons and got an MS in Library Science, learned how to bring us into the twenty-first century." We were looking out the window behind the row of shelves so we couldn't see the computers that replaced the card catalogue.

"It does look nice," said Rachel. "Especially the floors."

The floor was my favorite part of the library. It held a hundred and fifty year history like a well-kept artifact. Even the darkened lines that showed where pews had been when the building was still a church, before it was turned into a library, were still visible.

"They're hard pine and far more solid than anything built today. But you're not here to talk about the library."

"Like I said, I'm here for Mary's funeral and to find who killed Joseph."

A siren wail burst into the air outside, startling the birds at their seed cone. It sounded like an omen. Rachel cringed and began twisting her hair the way she did in high school when she was nervous. When the siren faded into whatever small town emergency drew it, she looked more closely at the photo of Nathan and Cathy.

"I recognize your house in this picture. Do your parents still live there?"

"Very much so."

"I liked them. They were good to Teddy and me when my mother died. I remember the doughnuts your father always bought on Saturdays."

"My mother gave up lecturing him about empty calories and his diabetes."

"Didn't we have doughnuts before we started our bike ride that day?"

I knew which day she meant. I only remembered that the sandwiches we packed for our lunches rotted at the bottom of our bike packs. Weeks later we unloaded them and threw them into the trash.

"My parents will be sorry to miss you. They're in Florida for the winter."

"Escaping New Hampshire's blizzards and coming back before hurricane season."

"This is their home." The birds returned to the seed cone and began feeding again. "I wish you'd move back."

"New Orleans is my home now. I own a house there, my paintings sell well in The French Quarter, and I have a following among the New Orleans' elite. Why would I come back to New Hampshire winters?"

"I'll take a blizzard over a hurricane like Katrina any time."

The door to the library opened, and a draft reached us. A man came in and found us behind the shelves. Teddy. Rachel stood up to greet her brother. He was tall and even thinner than Rachel. With hair that turned gray before he had reached thirty, I thought of him as the tin man. Wiry. Stiff, but flexible. The heavy parka he wore against the January cold covered muscles toned from running the farm he bought from Seth Thompson, even though Seth's barn had been the scene of Joseph's murder.

Outside, the church bells sounded twelve o'clock. They chimed three times a day. 8 a.m., noon, 8 p.m. Teddy nodded at me and managed to say "hello." He lifted Rachel's parka from the chair. It looked like he threw it at her. "You said noon. Janet has lunch for us." Without saying anything else, he went to the bulletin board where he checked that his wife's business card was still there. He tacked up a couple more cards, then went into the bathroom.

Teddy's wife helped him run his farm, ordering New Hampshire made–crafts and artisan food for the stand. She sold her own work there, handmade quilts that cost a month of my librarian's salary and were a bargain at that price. Rachel put on her parka and went to the bulletin board to look at Janet's card.

"Janet does well here," I said. "The town's accepted her."

"Even Seth Thompson?"

"I wouldn't go that far." I loved the irony that Seth sold his farm and the barn to Teddy before he knew that Teddy's wife was black. Seth hated what he called "the darkening" of New Hampshire, hated the Hispanic people who came from Nashua to buy summer produce. When the local teenagers started to go to dance or music or athletic camps instead of working in the fields in the summer, he was forced to hire Jamaican helpers with work visas.

Rachel took Janet's card off the bulletin board. "What about their daughter? She okay at the high school?"

"Elizabeth is as popular as Teddy. She was taking music lessons from Mary."

"I heard her play. She's good. Does she know about Joseph?" she asked as she tacked the card back up.

I glanced at Jody, who had come back to the checkout desk and was listening even as she was helping an elderly man. "She knows that he was found dead in the barn. I don't think she knows who found him or how he died."

I suspected that Elizabeth knew which teenagers still visited the barn that was in even worse shape now than when we were teenagers. Teddy ran a successful farm. He used the barn for storage and the hay he sold to backyard gardeners. But he had made no repairs to it. The wooden cow's head still looked down, judging the teenagers who snuck into it to have sex or to drink or to ingest the latest trendy drug. Rumors circulated that Teddy visited the barn at night and talked to Joseph.

When I heard the toilet flush, I went into my cubicle, put the photo of Nathan and Cathy back on my desk, and grabbed my parka. It was the same turquoise as Rachel's, but so ragged around the edges that some of the feathers kept finding their way out. I pulled my hat and gloves out of the sleeve. "I'll come outside with you." I signaled to Jody that I was going to lunch.

Teddy walked in front of us. Rachel took my hand and waited until he was outside. "Promise me you'll help find Joseph's killer."

"I will."

Jody and the man at the check out desk watched us leave. She was a good worker, but an even better gossip. I gave up all hope of keeping a reopened search secret.

A blast of air made colder by a biting wind greeted us outside the library. We'd have a storm before the end of the weekend. Rachel climbed in beside Teddy in his truck. He started to offer me a ride, but I waved him away. I needed to think about Mary's eulogy waiting at home for me to finish. I faced the wind to walk the half-mile up the hill to my house, convinced that Joseph's murder was a case as cold as the threatening weather.

2

THE HALF-MILE WALK from the library to my house hadn't changed since I was a kid. At least on the surface. The town hall that once held the library looked the same with its Civil War memorial in the front. Before I could read words, I used to find the letters in the names of the veterans the memorial commemorated. The church across the street looked the same, but it had fewer and fewer members despite being renamed the Shelby Community Church so it would appeal to more than committed Congregationalists. Even so, we'd been forced to rent the parsonage and to move to a part-time minister. Pastor Pam was good but not always available in a crisis. I couldn't imagine sitting down with her hour after hour the way I had with Reverend Tibbetts after Nathan and Cathy died.

I started up Spring Hill Road. Houses built in the nineteenth century lined the road except where a baseball field was used for boys' Little League and girls' softball. I loved the old days when boys and girls played Little League together. Rachel, Joseph, and I were all on the Mets. Our coach was Rachel's father, who taught me not to be afraid of the ball. I remembered a photo of Rachel and me posing in our uniforms, holding up our mitts, our cap brims turned to the back the way the big boys wore them. We won the game that day and her father treated us all to ice cream. A week later we learned that Rachel's mother had leukemia. It was the first we knew of sorrow.

Walking up the hill, I felt my eyes water in the wind. Everything looked desolate. The coming blizzard might create havoc with driving, but at least it would transform the landscape for a while, until traffic dirtied the snowbanks. When I passed Lucille Larcom's house, she was just getting out of her car, carrying a large object. She called to me. "Deborah, I found just the thing."

Lucille taught English and history at Shelby High School. Despite a few wrinkles around her eyes, she didn't look much older than when she was a first year teacher and all the boys had a crush on her. She worked out at a fancy health club in Milford, dyed and permed her reddish-brown hair so that it fell in soft waves to her shoulders, and dressed in clothes designed for twenty-year-olds. Strangers might peg her as a business executive or a real estate agent instead of a teacher. I suspected the current crop of boys still had a crush on her.

I walked into the short dirt space that served as her driveway. None of us who lived in Spring Hill Road's old houses had garages. We'd be breaking our backs shoveling and brushing off our cars by Monday. I stopped next to Lucille's car, my back against it so I could stay sheltered from the wind.

She showed me the large board encased in clear plastic that she was holding. "A magnetic board. I also got magnets. We can make a collage of all those photos we found at Mary's."

For years, I'd had a key to Mary's house across the street from mine, and she had one to my house. Whenever one of us was away, the other watered plants, brought in the mail, made sure the pipes didn't freeze if it was winter. When I went to Mary's after she died to rescue her cat, I brought Lucille with me. We sat there all afternoon going through photographs we'd found in decorative boxes on one of her bookshelves. We took out ones we wanted to display at her funeral, threw ones that were faded beyond recognition into a trash bag, and returned the others to the boxes. Lucille threw away twice as many as I did. "Maybe I'm too fussy," she said when I asked her about it.

Before we left Mary's, I found Beethoven sleeping on the couch as if he hadn't noticed that his owner was gone. I brought him home, knowing that I was destined to become the new owner of a ten-year-old cat covered in gray fur that would shed all over my house.

"This is perfect," I said to Lucille. "We went through all those photos and I never thought about how to display them."

"If you don't mind, I'll put them together and take them to the church this afternoon."

"That would be great. I'm stealing a little extra time for lunch so I can work on Mary's eulogy at home. It will help me to look out my window and see her house."

I left Lucille to unload whatever else was in her car. I liked her and she had been a support the last week, but there was a façade about her I never quite understood. Even when she was our high school teacher, she seemed to be hiding something behind her make-up.

My driveway was as primitive as Lucille's. I walked down it to my side door. Inside, the kitchen felt warm after the fifteen degrees outside. I draped my parka over a chair, stuffing my hat and gloves in its sleeve. In the basement below, the furnace rattled. A new one was on the list of repairs I needed, but it wouldn't happen until next fall. In the meantime, I did what I could to keep the heating bills down. The thermostat stayed at sixty-five degrees. If I put it lower, it took more oil to raise the temperature. I closed off two of the three upstairs bedrooms and used a woodstove in the living room to supplement the oil, whose price ranged from expensive to insane. I'd been foolish to buy a hundred-and-fifty-year-old house that was bigger than I'd ever need, but my love for the nineteenth century prevailed over my common sense.

In the living room, Beethoven uncurled himself from one of two chairs he'd already claimed as his own. Only a few embers glowed in the woodstove that the chairs faced. I stoked them and added a log. When it caught, I warmed my back at the flames. More than the weather chilled me. Rachel's appearance, and the distance I felt between us, had reopened the wounds left by Joseph's murder. Mary's house across the street already looked deserted.

Rachel and I will find our friendship again, I told myself as I went back into the kitchen. Beethoven followed me, stopped at his cat dish, and meowed. I knew Mary fed him only in the morning and the evening, but I refilled his dish with dry food. He was adjusting just like I was.

After I nuked a pot of leftover chili, I carried it back into the living room, remembering how Rachel and I sat at the parsonage that September of our senior year. We talked our hearts out with a minister who could offer no comfort. Reverend Tibbetts knew we had both walled ourselves off from the church. He didn't press us with prayers or reassurances that God had a purpose and that Joseph was in a better place. He tried to help us think through who could have killed him. Who would know he had gone to the barn? When we left, he said, "Don't add guilt to your sorrow." The same words he said to me when I was blaming myself for letting Nathan take our daughter for an ice cream cone.

I sat on the sofa I'd arranged with its back to the front window, set my chili on the coffee table, and picked up the Bible I kept there, tracing its gold lettering, and feeling the softness of its leather cover. I rarely read it, but I kept it in view to remind myself of how Reverend Tibbetts helped me find the good in religion after Nathan and Cathy died. I opened the Bible to the passage I kept marked with the thin cloth marker attached to the threading on the cover: John 14:27, one of the verses Reverend Tibbetts read at Joseph's funeral. "Peace I leave with you, my peace I give unto you… Let not your heart be troubled, neither let it be afraid." I'd been afraid then, and I was afraid now that I'd agreed to help Rachel search for Joseph's killer.

I put the Bible back down, managed a few bites of chili, then found the remote and clicked on the television I'd hung on the wall opposite the sofa. The weather channel would distract me from too many memories and a gnawing sense of guilt. The forecasters were going crazy. The storm barreling up from North Carolina would carry sixty-mile-per-hour winds and two to three feet of drifting snow. They delighted in their charts and their clichés like "barreling up." They seemed to revel in naming the first Nor'easter of the season, though this year, an unimaginative "Alfred." They would dramatize it for another two days before it hit on Monday, just in time for the morning commute. Plenty of time for people to raid the grocery stores, cancel their appointments, change their airplane flights. Teenagers would do what Rachel and I always did—ignore their homework. At least the storm would wait until after Mary's funeral. She'd been cremated, so no backhoe had to punch through the frozen ground to dig her grave, and no one would have to stand frozen next to it.

I clicked off the TV and went into the kitchen to put my half-eaten chili back into the refrigerator. Beethoven was just coming up from the cellar where I'd put his litter box, which forced me to leave the door open a crack. He brushed against my legs, then walked back to his chair in the living room.

A photo of Cathy sitting on her new tricycle stopped me. She was holding tight to the handlebars and wearing a black and white polka dot shirt. She smiled in the way she had when she was proud and a little frightened, her baby teeth showing, her blue eyes wide open. I'd kept that photo on a refrigerator ever since she died, first when I came back to Shelby to live with my parents. It followed me to my room in Boston when I went to Simmons. I always kept a few photos on my refrigerator, rotating ones of Nathan, of my parents, of spring flowers or fall foliage or mist on my tomato plants. But always this picture of Cathy.

The reason hit me like the cold air when I opened the refrigerator door. It was like that September day in 1990 when Rachel and I propped our bicycles under the watchful eyes of the wooden cow and found Joseph, his blue eyes wide open in death.

If I tried to erase Cathy's death by removing the photo, I was afraid I'd erase her memory. I went through the living room and climbed the stairway that rose steeply to the second floor to find photos that would give me ideas for Mary's eulogy. The door to my bedroom stood open. My bed was made. No clothes lay scattered on it or on the floor. Even the books on my nightstand were piled neatly with my reading glasses resting on top of them. Nathan had been a clutterer. Now, I controlled my emotions by controlling my own clutter.

The house was old, the closets few and tiny. I opened the only one in the room across the hall from my bedroom. I pulled out a plastic storage container and rummaged through diplomas, textbooks I should give to the library's annual book sale, shoe boxes of faded photographs. At the bottom, I found what I wanted. Two of Shelby High School's yearbooks. *The Cavalier*, 1990 and 1991, with my name, Deborah Madison, printed on top of both. I hadn't thought of myself as Deborah Madison in years. I was Deborah Strong, convincing myself that the cliché was true. What doesn't kill you makes you stronger.

Repacking the boxes with everything except the yearbooks and pushing them back into the closet, I didn't feel strong. The books felt as heavy as my memories when I carried them to my desk. Outside the window, Mary's house looked forlorn. The maple tree in her front yard was empty of leaves, and her flower bed on the side was an arrangement of sticks.

I turned away from its emptiness to page through the 1990 yearbook, skipping to photos labeled "Coming Attractions" with candids of our junior class. Me standing in front of a chalkboard, my hair parted to the side, thick, short, and flipped off my forehead in the style I still wore. I must have been giving a presentation because I wore a skirt and blouse. With my oversized plastic glasses and one arm angled onto my hip, I looked decidedly schoolmarmish.

The candid of Rachel showed her with a band tied around her brow, her arms over her head, palms together, squatting her legs into a V. I remembered Joseph taking the photo and telling her to pose like the Egyptian we all said she looked like. Joseph's candid overlapped hers. I'd forgotten how handsome he was. Blond hair, wavy and combed loosely above his eyes, a dimple showing at the side of his wide grin. He was sitting at a desk in what must have been the chemistry lab because he was holding a beaker, toasting Rachel who had taken his photo.

Beethoven appeared at the door of the room I had kept closed off to him. I wanted to keep him out, keep this room free of his cat hair, but I let him investigate while I opened our 1991 *Cavalier*. I tensed myself for what I knew I'd find. The dedication page to Joseph James Wheeler, 1973–1990. His blue eyes stared at me as if they had come alive again. Like most of us, he had his senior photo taken in the summer by a local photographer who shot photos outside in natural light. He was leaning casually against a tree, his arms folded, the collar of his blue shirt slightly askew. We paid extra to have this the only color photo in the yearbook. On the opposite page were a half dozen black and white photos: Joseph showing off his hula hoop skills when we were in elementary school; crossing the finish line at a junior high track meet; posing with Rachel at the junior prom, looking more uncomfortable than dapper; that same photo of him in the chemistry lab toasting with a beaker. Under the last photo of him straddling the branch of a birch tree in front of the school was a reference to a Robert Frost poem. "In loving memory of Joseph, our swinger of birches."

Beethoven jumped onto my desk and tried to sit on the yearbook. "Oh, no you don't," I said as I picked him up and put him on the floor. He sniffed around then jumped onto the bed and settled down for a nap.

I looked back at Joseph's memorial page. Math Club. National Honor Society. Jazz Band. Basketball. Baseball. Rachel had removed Joseph's caricature from the collage she had drawn of our class and put it in the corner of the memorial page. She drew him standing, legs apart, an arm raised in farewell. A dialogue balloon floated above him, empty of words. Kudos from Joseph's teachers were written between the photos. I read the one by Lucille Larcom. "Joseph was a gift to Shelby High School, a Renaissance man with a bright future."

I turned to the back page photos of the teachers. Lucille looked as young as Joseph when she was team-teaching American Studies with Conrad Donaldson. Donaldson's son, Eric, was the same age as us and one of Joseph's best friends. Five years later when Lucille married Eric, no one commented about their age difference.

I flipped back to the memorial page of the yearbook and Lucille's comment. Something she said when we were choosing the selections for Mary's funeral nagged. Whatever connection I was about to make disappeared when my cell phone rang. I said my simple "Hello."

"It's me."

Rachel. We used to joke about how we identified ourselves. "Hi, me."

"You remember."

"Of course. I've been looking through our old yearbooks. Thinking of how to bring Joseph into Mary's eulogy."

"Come pick me up and we'll go to dinner. I need to get away from Teddy and his farm. Too many ghosts. Bring the yearbook."

I looked again at the page dedicated to Joseph. The yearbook wouldn't help us find his killer. "I'll pick you up at six."

"Perfect."

She didn't say goodbye. Silence hung heavy in the air as nagging as our lost connection. My cuckoo clock sounding two broke the silence. I lifted Beethoven off the bed. He was a heavy cat, his fur soft and warm. Maybe his company would be worth the extra vacuuming. I closed the door behind us and let him walk down the stairs to his spot by the woodstove. I checked the fire before I went into the kitchen for my parka. Zipping it, I thought again of how the turquoise matched Rachel's jacket, a bridge to the friendship we had lost.

Outside, my breath formed a cloud in the freezing air. The wind penetrated the back of my parka. When I passed her house, Lucille was putting the metallic board in her car. One of the photos she had attached escaped. I rescued it before it reached the road. Joseph and Rachel, arms around each other at Shelby Lake. They could have been models for a bathing suit company. Rachel's dark hair was wet and glistening and just touching Joseph's shoulder. Her yellow bikini highlighted her tanned skin. Joseph's hair was bleached by the sun into a shade almost as yellow. Both their bodies were lean and fit with the freshness of youth.

I brushed off the photo and carried it to Lucille. "I don't think you should use this one."

"Why not?" She glanced at the photo I still held.

"I took it the last summer Joseph was alive. It will hurt Rachel to see it."

She grabbed the photo from my hand. "Rachel's here?"

"She is. She came for Mary's funeral."

"That's a surprise."

"Maybe you didn't know that Rachel's mother died and her father was an alcoholic. Mary was like a mother to her and Teddy."

"All the teachers knew that. I'm just surprised that Rachel still cares. She was always a hard one."

I defended my friend. "Private, not hard."

"You sound like Mary. She often told me I misread Rachel. I said she was only defending her because she was Joseph's girlfriend."

"Whatever you thought then, forget it. Rachel's here for the funeral and I'd like you not to use this photo."

She opened her car door, put in the board, and let the photo of Joseph and Rachel fall onto the floor. "I'll fill in with something else. Want a ride?"

"Thanks anyway, but I need the walk." I left Lucille to get into her car, thinking of what she had written. "He was a gift to Shelby High School." He was also the only boy who didn't have a crush on her. At least that's what he said. I shook away the idea that any of the boys' crushes had been more than that when we were in high school.

3

I CROSSED THE street at Seth Thompson's. When he sold his
farm to Teddy, he bought a small house next to the church and
became the church and the library custodian. He painted the house
barn red, more, I thought, to thumb his nose at the white paint of
historic Shelby than in any nostalgia for his farm. I rather liked the
splash of color it provided.

A car slowed on the town hall side of the street. The driver rolled
down the window and called, "Deborah. It's freezing outside. Want
a ride?"

Susan Warner from Graniteville. I waved her on, then wished I
hadn't even though I was just a few steps from the library. I knew
that Susan had actually solved three murders since she had retired
from teaching at Souhegan University. I was tempted to ask for her
help with our cold case, but she wouldn't want to be involved with
another murder. I'd call her later if I thought she might remember
something. Joseph's death terrified our classmates from Graniteville
as much as it terrified the ones from Shelby.

Jody stood with Seth Thompson on the ramp at the side of the
library. I'd been gone longer than I anticipated. She was closing up,
and Seth had arrived for the couple of hours he spent cleaning on
Friday afternoons.

When Seth went into the library, she walked toward me. "I

thought you were coming back right after lunch."

I ignored her accusatory tone. I rarely left during library hours even for lunch. But I spent well over the forty hours of my contract inside the library, reading reviews, ordering books, arranging programs, dealing with the constant requests of the part-time clerks to change their schedules. The trustees didn't ask me to punch a clock. "Sorry, Jody. I intended to come back, but I got involved in writing Mary Wheeler's eulogy."

"I don't know how she survived when Joseph was murdered. Are you and— "

I cut her off before she could ask about Rachel and me trying to find Joseph's killer. "Will you be at the funeral tomorrow?"

"It's my Saturday to work. Can you ask one of the other clerks to take my place?"

"I'll try." I suspected she only thought about the funeral after hearing Rachel and me talk.

Inside the library, Seth was already upstairs running the vacuum cleaner in the children's area.

At the suggestion box, I took out three cards that had been deposited in it. I draped my parka, hat, and gloves over the nearest radiator. They'd be warm when I went back outside. I put on the sweater I kept at the chair in my always too-cold cubicle, and woke up my computer to look at the list of clerks. I called Jenny Burgess first. She was happy for the extra hours. Jody could attend the funeral and gawk at everyone there so she could speculate about who might have killed Joseph nearly thirty years ago.

The first suggestion card asked for some comfortable cushions. Anyone who wanted could put them on chairs that were too hard for some of the older patrons. The woman who wrote the second card complained about the rug under the table in the children's area. It was never clean enough. Before I looked at the third card, I went upstairs to talk with Seth. He was vacuuming around the children's table but not under it. He was a big man, still powerful from his years as a farmer. His glasses were Coke-bottle-thick, and he often left dust on the shelves and bunnies on the floor. His definition of "clean" wasn't my own. When he saw me, he turned off the vacuum cleaner and used his foot to press the cord retract button.

"Didn't hear you. All cleaned for this week." He spoke with the heavy accent of a native born into Yankee New Hampshire eighty years ago. Dropped r's and g's, double syllables for a one syllable word, clipped sentences.

I handed him the complaint card. He scowled at it and handed it back. "Impossible to keep it clean with all those kids. It'll be a mess next week. There's a blizzard comin'. Won't nobody care if there's a bit of dirt on the floor."

Seth was an intelligent man. I suspected he butchered his grammar to defy the newcomers in town with what he called their fancy college degrees. "Just get those couple of dust bunnies under the table. This woman who complained always comes in on Saturdays with two kids. She'll look and then stay quiet for awhile."

"I s'pose you won't be here. Goin' to that funeral?"

"Yes, of course. I've known Mary since I was a kid."

"Won't be at the funeral. Didn't like that woman."

"I know, and I've never understood why." I'd tried for years to soften Seth's animosity toward Mary.

"Should've done a better job with her kid. He had no business poking around in my barn." This was the most he had ever said to me about it.

"Joseph and I were friends. He wasn't one of the kids who hung out in your barn."

"Don't matter. He got killed there and the police searched my farm. Treated me like a killer. Somethin' like that happens, cops you grew up with turn against you."

"They searched my house, too."

"Probably was one of you teenagers killed that kid. Wasn't me."
Seth's voice was controlled, but his face spoke the fury he must
have been burying ever since the murder. He moved the kids'
chairs away from the table and started vacuuming again as if he
were sucking up memories along with the dust bunnies.

I went back to my desk to look at the next card. A request, not a
complaint this time. An avid mystery reader had moved to Shelby
from some place on the West Coast. She wanted me to order the
latest books in the series written by three of her favorite authors.
I looked up each of the series on Amazon, though I wouldn't
order from there. Carole T. Beers wrote Pepper Kane mysteries
about horse shows. I checked it as a yes on the list the woman
sent me. I did the same for the other two, Michael Niemann's
international thrillers about UN investigator Valentin Vermeulen,
and Clive Rosengren's Hollywood mysteries featuring Eddie
Collins, sometime actor, sometime PI. If half our patrons were
going to read only mysteries, at least they could move into new,
unfamiliar territory.

My cell phone rang just as Seth started cleaning downstairs. It
was Lucille. "Deborah. Finish up at the library and come to the
church so I can show you how I set everything up."

I recoiled at Lucille's demanding tone. She always reminded
me of Lucille Ball shrieking at Desi Arnaz on re-runs of *I Love
Lucy*, even though Lucy was more obsequious to her Cuban
American husband than demanding. But I was ready to leave the
library anyway. "I'll be there in a few. I'm being driven out by Seth
Thompson's vacuuming."

"He's a creep. You shouldn't be alone with him."

"He's harmless." I hung up the phone and glanced at Seth's
broad back and his thinning gray hair that needed washing. He
wore one of the T-shirts he cleaned in, no matter the weather,
and jeans a little too tight around his heavy rear end. He was a

man locked in the past, resentful of the present, likely afraid of the future when his body would begin to fail him. Even though his anger had infiltrated the entire library, I'd never thought of him as dangerous.

He turned off the vacuum cleaner when he saw me. "Goin' to meet that sister of Teddy's? What's her name?"

"Rachel."

"You and her should let that cold case stay cold. Don't do no one any good to rake up the past."

Jody had done what I thought she'd do: told the first of what I knew would be many that Rachel was here to find Joseph's murderer. "Clean well," I said as I pulled on my parka and started toward the church. My words were drowned out by the whirring of the vacuum cleaner.

The wind had quieted and the cold air felt good after the stuffiness of the library. Across the street, Irwin Trombly was walking the German Shepherd he'd outfitted in a woolen wrap against the cold. Rufus was pulling him along so hard, Irwin almost lost his footing. I waved then hurried on. Irwin was fifty and fit and good-looking in a middle-aged-man sort of way. Despite his quiet advances, he didn't ignite my sexual desire. It died with Nathan. If it ever returned, I'd welcome it, but I felt no urgency.

I opened the side door of the church and stepped into the silence. Lucille wasn't in the function room where we'd hold the reception after Mary's funeral, so I climbed the stairs to the sanctuary. She was sitting in the front pew. When she heard me, she stood up.

"It's empty." She gestured to the communion table that had been moved three steps down from the chancel where I'd deliver the eulogy.

"Pastor Pam has Mary's ashes. She'll arrange the table with the urn and a photo and flowers." I'd been with Pam when the ashes arrived, watched her take Mary's wedding ring out of the plastic bag taped to the urn and slip the ring inside. We prayed silently for the loss of our friend.

Lucille's voice shrieked into the quiet of the sanctuary. "Did you look at what I arranged downstairs?"

"Not yet. Come down and show me."

We descended the stairs to the function room together. I long ago lost count of the events I'd gone to there. Bean suppers in February, town meeting suppers in March. Easter pancake breakfasts after sunrise service. Game dinners in October. After Mary's funeral tomorrow, we'd break bread together here as we'd done after so many funerals and the occasional wedding. The room would be filled with the aroma of soups that the church's Kindness Krew would prepare to serve to the mourners. Most of them were mourners themselves.

I walked over to the table where Lucille had set up photographs of Mary next to a guest book opened for people to sign. A few framed photos surrounded the book. Lucille had placed Mary's 1991 school photo next to Joseph's. Mother and son leaned separately in twin poses against the photographers' ubiquitous tree. On the metallic frame that Lucille had rested against a beam, snapshots formed a collage as if they were on a refrigerator.

"The photos look nice, Lucille. You found a good way to prop up the board."

"There's no relative to take the guest book."

"I know." I ran my finger over the snapshots on the bulletin board. "I wonder who took some of these photos."

"Mary took most of the ones of Joseph."

I fingered a photo of our American Studies class. I had chosen it. Lucille and Conrad Donaldson stood on either side of the team-taught class. Lucille looked as young as the students. "How long ago this seems. We were such innocents. I thought history only happened to the long-dead. I suppose we're part of the history of Shelby High School now. Do you ever think of our class, or do all the new students manage to wipe out the old?"

"I try not to think of your class."

"Because of Joseph?"

"No. He was a gift to Shelby High School."

That phrase again. "You wrote that next to his memorial picture in the yearbook."

Lucille turned away from the photos and faced me. "You remember that far back?"

"I looked at the yearbook when I was writing Mary's eulogy."

"I don't remember much about that year." She looked at the photo. "You were a good-looking class. So much potential."

I gestured toward a photo of Joseph, Teddy, and Eric in their baseball uniforms, high-fiving after winning some long-forgotten game. "Do you ever hear from Eric? Teddy stays in touch. Says he's done really well with some West Coast investment firm."

"Never hear from him. Never think of him. He was a mistake from the beginning."

I'd heard her utter that phrase before, so this wasn't the first time I wondered if the "beginning" was high school, or later when Lucille and Eric married. I looked again at the baseball photo. "Didn't Eric's father coach the baseball team?"

"He did."

"Do you ever see him? You both run in history circles."

"See Conrad? Not if I can avoid it. He didn't help me when we taught American Studies. And he certainly didn't welcome me into the family when I married Eric."

The church furnace turned on, its initial rattle echoing in the emptiness and making me aware of how cold the room was. I remembered the American Studies classroom. Conrad had always complained that it was too hot, and Lucille wrapped herself in a sweater she kept on a chair. "I thought you were both good teachers."

"I'd think of an idea and Conrad would dismiss it. 'Not another of those stories of unrecovered women who should stay unrecovered,' he'd say."

"Aren't you descended from one?"

"Distantly. Lucy Larcom. She was one of the girls who worked in the Lowell Mills. Became a key writer for their magazine, *The Lowell Offering*. She never married. Maybe that's why she was able to become a poet and to write a memoir of her days in the mill."

"I remember that memoir. It made me see so clearly what it was like to go to the mills when she was only, what, thirteen?"

"Just eleven. She survived. She thrived. Just like we'll do."

"I'm sorry things were difficult when you started teaching. We gave other first-year teachers a hard time, but never you."

"Like I said, 'We'll survive.' Mary's death has just opened old wounds, that's all."

I scanned through the photos. There were none of Joseph and Rachel together. I shivered from more than the cold. *He was a gift.* I pushed away my suspicion that Lucille's comment connected somehow to Joseph's death. "We're all reliving the past. Old wounds will heal," I lied. Death invaded the living like a wound that began to heal, only to open up again like a festering sore.

Lucille lifted her parka from a chair she'd hung it on. If she used to be cold in her high school classroom, she must have been freezing in the church without it. "You're right," she said. "I'll feel better after tomorrow. I'm going home. Want a ride?"

"No thanks. I like the walk."

"Even in the cold?"

"*Especially* in the cold." I followed Lucille outside and walked toward home as if the cold compress of the January air could heal my heart.

When I reached my door, I took off my boots in the kitchen and went into the living room to hang my parka over the woodstove. Beethoven jumped off his chair and rubbed against my ankles.

I bent to pet him. "You're a good watch cat, Beethoven." I put a log on the fire, unable to shake off the feeling that I might have buried some memory that would lead Rachel and me to whatever happened that day so many years ago.

My eyes rested on the laptop I kept on a bookcase. I was a librarian, a researcher, someone able to find any record of Joseph's death if any record existed. I took the computer off of its shelf and rested it on my lap. Shelby's tiny, stapled-together bi-weekly papers from the 1980s wouldn't be digitized, but maybe the Nashua *Telegraph* or the Manchester *Union Leader* were. I Googled both and found nothing. Newspapers were as stingy with their digitizing as the state was with its fund for education. No cold case records lurked on the Shelby Police Department website. If I stopped at the station to ask, I'd be met with blank stares from a police force so young they were in diapers when Joseph was murdered. Rachel and I needed to start this alone. If we found anything, we could involve the police later.

I couldn't wait brooding in the house until it was time to get Rachel, so I put on my jacket, left some food for Beethoven, and closed the kitchen door just as the cuckoo clock sounded four. I drove to the road at the corner of Teddy's farm stand and followed it to Lake Shelby. Already, it was turning dark. I got out of my car and walked to the picnic table on the beach. A few bob houses dotted the frozen lake. Only the dim light of a rising moon shown through the overcast sky.

Rachel and Teddy's father had loved ice fishing. He'd take us to the lake when we were kids. If a snowstorm covered the ice, we'd shovel a rink. Rachel skated as fast as the boys, gliding along the ice while I skated slowly and tentatively. Sometimes Mr. Cummings would stop fishing long enough to play hockey with us. Until he no longer fished and only sat in his bob house drinking.

A whippoorwill started to whistle from the grove of trees. It stopped, flew to the opposite side of the beach, its dark shape and my memories making me think of a hockey puck. Could Rachel and Teddy's father be the person who hit Joseph? A hockey puck wasn't a ball, but its edges were round. It hadn't been in the news reports, but we all knew Joseph's fall against the wheelbarrow had made it hard to identify the weapon. Shelby was a small town. People talked. Even the police. I shook off the idea and walked back to my car. Rachel and Teddy had enough sorrow. Their father needed to rest in peace.

4

THE ROAD TO Teddy's farm was frozen solid and rutted. Dark had engulfed it so completely that if I didn't know there was a barn with a cow's head peeking from the rafters, I would have missed it. Opposite the barn were fields and housing that Teddy had built for his Jamaican workers the year after he bought the place. They were heatless and boarded up for the winter, but better than the shacks Seth Thompson grudgingly provided his workers. Tonight they were invisible. When I reached the farmhouse, Rachel appeared beneath the porch light before I turned off my motor. Behind her, Janet said something and held out a hat and scarf. She waved at me before she closed the door. Rachel pulled the hat over her ears, wrapped the scarf around her neck, and zipped her jacket.

I leaned across the seat to open the door. Under the car's interior light, I recognized the multi-colored blues of her hat and scarf as a matching set Teddy's daughter had knitted. I touched the edge of the scarf that felt more familiar to me than this friend who had disappeared from my life. "Elizabeth must like you. She's been wearing these to youth group for the last two months."

"She's like we were in high school. Worried about her clothes, too interested in who's dating who, angry at an assignment. Actually, she's worse than we were. Today's social media would have destroyed me."

"She's not as bad as some of the kids I see."

"She's sweet, but I had to get out of there. She keeps asking what Joseph was like. I don't think she knows how he died. Janet tells us not to bring up the past, and all Teddy does is silence me if I ask him something about Mary or Joseph." She pulled the scarf so tight, I feared she'd strangle herself. "Teddy forgets that we were at their house so much because our mother was dead and our father was falling apart. I don't know how I'll last until my flight home next Saturday."

I turned to back the car out of the driveway, wanting to say, "*This is your home.*" The yearbook on the back seat reminded me of the empty room in my house. "You could stay with me this week."

"That would help."

I wanted to find our friendship again instead of getting caught up in a futile search for a killer from thirty years ago. I wondered if she told Teddy why she had come home. "Maybe not a good idea. Teddy and Janet would be offended. Judging from that hat and scarf you're wearing, Elizabeth would be, too."

"At least give me tomorrow after the funeral. I'll think of an excuse. Sunday I'll stay with you again to escape the blizzard."

"Promise me you'll go back to Teddy's on Monday as soon as the roads are plowed. Accept the life your brother made for himself."

"He's repressing the past."

"And you're reliving it. Bury your demons."

"Stop here."

The barn loomed on the right the side of the road, barely visible in the dark. I braked and put the car into park without pulling to the side. "It's so dark I can't even see the cow's head."

"Why is there a cow's head there anyway? Seth Thompson didn't have cows."

"I asked my parents once. He inherited the farm and a few dairy cows from his father. Some law was passed at the time that said he would have to use stanchions instead of stalls if he sold milk."

"Stanchions?"

"Those metal things cows get enclosed in when they're not ranging outside. He refused and sold the cows. My parents told me there were only four or five."

Whenever I drove past the barn in daylight, the cow seemed to be watching. Once, I asked Teddy why he didn't take it down. He mumbled something about the cow knowing everything and changed the subject. Even in tonight's dark, I could feel its accusing eyes.

I put the car into gear to drive away.

"Wait," said Rachel. "We need to go inside."

"Whatever for?"

Her voice cracked. "Clues to Joseph's murder."

"There won't be any clues after all these years."

"I just need to see it again, do what you said, bury my ghost. Finally get it to stop infiltrating my paintings."

I put my car into neutral with my foot on the brake. "It's too dark. Your ghost can wait. Unless Teddy has electricity in there, we won't see anything. It'll be freezing. The dirt floor will be solid with frost."

"Indulge me, Deborah. We can buy headlamps."

Rachel said my name the way she did when we were kids and she wanted her way. If I delayed her, maybe she'd at least wait until daylight. "First, we eat."

"Not Skip's. That's the last place I saw Joseph."

"Skip's closed years ago. Shelby has no restaurant now."

A small animal crossed in front of my headlights, chased by a fisher cat. Whatever the cat was hunting was as cloaked in the dark as Joseph's ghost.

"What was that?"

"A fisher cat, chasing something. It might live in the barn," I said, though I had no idea where fisher cats lived.

"Take me anywhere for dinner," said Rachel as I pulled the car forward. "As long as we go past a store where we can buy headlamps."

"There's a new restaurant on 101. It only sells chowder. A bowl will warm the bottoms of our toes."

"New England style. Remember how good Mary's was?" The defensive edge Rachel wore all through our senior year softened at the memory.

"Probably the same recipe my mother uses."

"101 has all those box stores, doesn't it? We can stop for headlamps first."

I no more wanted to go into the barn in the frigid dark than I wanted to reopen the wounds left by Joseph's murder. "Can't it wait until after the funeral? When it's light. And maybe a little warmer."

"With a *blizzard* outside. I want to go before the service. Face Joseph's ghost before I mourn his mother." Rachel wasn't going to forget about the barn tonight.

I turned on my high beams to lead me along the dirt road. When we reached the paved roads at Teddy's farm stand, I dimmed them, even though we passed only a few cars. I turned into the flood of lights on Route 101, box stores, restaurants, and a line of cars filled with shoppers stocking up ahead of the predicted storm. I chose the first store on 101 likely to sell headlamps. A Walmart, its parking lot full.

"Which entrance?" I said as we got out of the car. Four stretched out ahead of us. "Outdoor Living. Sporting Goods. Home and Pharmacy. Groceries."

"I don't shop at Walmart. I'd guess Home and Pharmacy."

We followed a line of people into the store. Every customer at the checkout counters had placed batteries on the belt. I never understood why people waited for a storm to supply themselves. My cabinet was filled with double-As, triple-As, and Ds. They were stacked on a shelf under the beeswax candles that I liked to burn in the winter. I didn't really need to be quite so well stocked. I knew I had become excessively anal after Nathan and Cathy died. As if neatness could control life.

We wandered through five aisles before we gave up and asked where they stocked headlamps. Sporting goods. We found the right aisles. They were loaded with sleds, skis, skates, and sleeping bags good to zero degrees. Everything out in the open except the guns and ammunition. I was glad that cabinet was locked. When we found the headlamps, we read through the specs and bought two, each costing $22, batteries included.

"I hate this place," said Rachel.

"You've never been here."

"It's Walmart. We could be anywhere in the country. Same stores. Same movie theaters. Same chain restaurants."

I followed Rachel out of sporting goods. "Has New Orleans escaped all that?"

"Not the outskirts. But we've got the French Quarter and the River Walk. No chain stores allowed. That's why I'm able to sell my paintings without competing with cheesy reproduction prints."

I shared her opinion but didn't want to make a scene in a store where so many people stretched their limited dollars. "Need anything else while we're here?"

"Gloves. Elizabeth loaned me a hat and scarf, but my hands have been freezing."

We found the clothing section next to the grocery aisles. Rachel picked out some imitation leather gloves, and we chose the shortest line at the checkout counter. When we were second in line, the man in front of us began unloading a full cart. Packaged cookies, gallon-sized soft drinks, boxes of macaroni and cheese and Hamburger Helper. Food emptied, he lifted a large container of ice melt and a snow shovel onto the counter. At the bottom of his cart were a flashlight and batteries. He'd need to make two or three stops and spend more to buy the same items elsewhere.

He waited for the checkout clerk to load everything except the ice melt and shovel into plastic bags. The line kept lengthening behind us when he asked her to wait while he got ice from the freezer in front of the counters. She rang up the purchases while he figured out whether to slide his credit card or put it into the chip reader. It didn't go through, so he fumbled in his wallet to find a different one. Beside me, I could see Rachel impatiently shifting around her headlamp and gloves. Finally the man left, slowly pushing his cart and ignoring how the handle of his shovel nearly hit a woman carrying a baby.

We deposited our headlamps and gloves onto the counter. The clerk looked at the line that had formed and glanced at her watch. She smiled when we paid cash and refused the plastic bag.

"Long day?" I said.

She handed me the receipt. "Always like this before a storm. At least I get overtime."

I crumpled the receipt without looking at it. "Stay safe." I tossed the receipt into the trash can at the store entrance, found gloves and car keys in my purse, and walked with Rachel back into the parking lot where a train of cars was circling to find the closest spot to the entrance.

Rachel dropped the headlamps into the back seat. "That was awful. The malling of America. Worst thing that ever happened to our country."

Part of me agreed, even though I knew Walmarts provided low costs and convenience. The woman who checked us out might be tired but she had her overtime.

I drove another mile on 101, hitting the next traffic light when it was green. Just beyond it, a sign with a logo showing a steaming bowl announced Clive's Chowder House. It always made me think of *Moby-Dick*, the chapter called "Chowder" when Ishmael and Queequeg arrive in Nantucket and are offered "clam or cod." They ate both. And a steamy, savory treat it was. Clive's served clam, haddock, a mix of seafood, and a lobster stew so rich I couldn't eat a full bowl. All good, all expensive because of the near collapse of the New England fisheries. Atlantic cod was so over-fished, it wasn't on the menu any longer. The chowders came with bread baked in-house, white, sourdough, or whole wheat. Judging from the parking lot, plenty of people were willing to pay fifteen to twenty dollars, twenty-eight for the lobster stew.

I waited for a spot near the restaurant exit where an older couple were getting into their car. The same logo of a steaming chowder bowl decorated the exit door. I parked and retrieved the yearbooks from the back seat. We found the entrance, painted with the logo. Just inside the entryway stood a reproduction of Gloucester's fisherman's statue, its bronze fake, but its image of a fisherman holding onto a ship's wheel and staring out to sea accurate. Clive's statue even included the granite slab beneath the fisherman and the inscription

THEY THAT GO
DOWN TO THE SEA
IN SHIPS
1623 – 1923

Instead of looking out to sea, the statue beckoned us into a room whose walls were painted with murals of fish and fishermen.

"No mistaking this for Arnaud's," said Rachel.

"Don't get all New Orleans snobby. Unless you've forgotten your New England roots, you'll appreciate the food."

There were only booths, no tables, in Clive's. A hostess wearing a shirt designed with images of fish and lobsters led us to a vacant one in a corner by a window frosted with the cold. The hostess left us with a laminated one-page menu. I set the yearbooks at the end of the booth and slipped out of my parka, stuffing my hat and gloves into the sleeve.

"I like your trick." Rachel shoved her new gloves and the hat and scarf Elizabeth loaned her into her parka's sleeve, and then reached for the yearbooks.

I moved her hand. "Let's order first."

She looked at her menu. "Only four items and I still don't know what to choose. Do you have a favorite?"

"I live on a librarian's salary, so I don't often get the lobster stew. I'd spring for it tonight if you want. It's a special occasion."

"I live on an artist's earnings, so let's save that. We'll come back after we find out who killed Joseph."

A waiter appeared at the table, wearing a shirt with the same pattern as the hostess's. He filled our water glasses. "Drinks to start?"

Rachel took the drink list from where it rested between salt and pepper shakers shaped like lobster claws. "A bottle or a glass of wine?"

"One glass of the BV sauvignon blanc. I'm the driver."

She returned the drink list to the claws. "Make that two."

The waiter wrote down the drinks. "Are you ready to order or shall I come back?"

Rachel handed him her menu. "Clam chowder for me, with sourdough bread."

I gave him my menu. "I'll have the same except with whole wheat bread."

When he left, Rachel began twisting a strand of her hair. I opened the yearbook to the In Memoriam page and slid it to her. She continued to play with her hair as she studied the page. She didn't look up until the waiter arrived with our wine. "He was so young."

I tasted my wine. It was light, citrus flavored with a crisp finish. Nathan taught me about wine, taught me how to find good varieties that we could afford. BV was one of our favorites. "Drink in remembrance of me," I thought whenever I sipped it.

Rachel turned to her senior picture. I looked at it upside down. She was leaning against the same tree the photographer used for Joseph's picture. She read me what she had chosen for underneath her photo. "'Today, the road all runners come / Shoulder-high we bring you home / And set you at your threshold down / Townsman of a stiller town.'—A. E. Housman. 'How can the dead be truly dead when they still live in the souls of those who are left behind?'—Carson McCullers."

Her quotations were about Joseph, not herself. Our chowder arrived before I could say something about her choices. She turned the pages back to the photo of Eric Donaldson, taken in some photographer's studio instead of in the natural outdoor light favored by so many of us. She closed the book and pushed it aside to make room for her chowder. "Whatever happened to Eric? And his dad?"

I blew on my first spoonful of chowder. "I remember you at the prom with Eric. Mr. Donaldson was one of the chaperones."

"I've blocked out that night. I kept thinking I should have been with Joseph."

"I can't even remember who I went with."

"Stanley Lewis. Biggest nerd in the class."

"No wonder I forgot. But I remember my dress. Orange, strapless, flounced at my knees." It was the year most of the girls rejected the black gowns that had been fashionable the year before and opted for color. Rachel wore a neon green scoop-necked dress with long strands of silver fringe that swayed just above her knees. She looked gorgeous, a cross between Cleopatra and a Fitzgerald flapper. She and Eric were chosen King and Queen. When they danced together after their crowning, Rachel cried on his shoulder. The rest of the night she danced with each of the boys, babbling in a kind of manic high. Exhausted, she asked Eric to take her home instead of to the post prom party.

Rachel spoke reluctantly. "Mr. Donaldson taught American Studies with Miss Larcom. Eric liked her. He kept talking about her all night. Missing Joseph wasn't the only reason I had such a horrible time."

"They got married."

Rachel stirred her chowder. "You're right. This chowder is wonderful."

I wondered why Rachel didn't react when I said they had married. "Eric and Lucille Larcom. Not his father and Lucille."

Rachel tasted the bread. "This sourdough is as good as the chowder."

While we worked through our bowls of chowder, I told her the story of Lucille and Eric's marriage. She kept eating and sipping her wine. She seemed uninterested in hearing about a teacher marrying a former student.

Rachel put down her spoon and opened the yearbook to the faculty page and Lucille's photo. "I never liked her."

"She was young then. She became a good friend of Mary's. We worked together on tomorrow's service."

"I guess people change." Rachel closed the yearbook.

I rested my hand on top of hers. "We've *all* changed."

She moved her hand away. "What was it we used to say? 'Ever the best of friends.'"

"From *Great Expectations.*" I hoped she was right. I moved the yearbook aside. "On Joseph's memorial page, Lucille wrote that he was a gift to Shelby High School. Do you know why she would write that?"

Rachel stared at me over her wine glass as she finished the last swallow. She put it down and broke off a piece of bread. "I have no idea. Joseph didn't like her. I don't know why she'd call him a gift."

"Do you think she was sleeping with Eric and Joseph knew it?"

"That would be statutory rape. Was she that stupid?"

"Hormones trump intelligence."

"It doesn't matter. Let's talk about something else. I'm here to find Joseph's killer, not to talk about old teachers."

If Rachel wanted to tell me anything that involved Lucille and Joseph, she wasn't ready tonight. "I don't know where to start a search. We should at least wait until daylight."

Rachel insisted again. "The barn will trigger memories. Maybe something we noticed but forgot about."

I tilted my bowl to get the last spoonful of chowder. "We can watch at the service tomorrow."

Rachel pushed away her bowl. "For what?"

"Someone who looks uncomfortable." Rachel then closed the yearbook. "Someone who doesn't want to remember that Mary had a son."

"Someone we'll be surprised to see at the funeral."

The waiter arrived and asked us if we wanted dessert. We declined, and I insisted on paying. Rachel grabbed the yearbooks. We hadn't looked through them as much as I thought we would.

We walked to the car, passing a couple speaking English heavily accented with a German inflection. The man wanted to be sure he could order beer with his chowder. The belly protruding from his unzipped jacket suggested he should forget the beer.

In the car, Rachel turned on the radio. "Nice station. Classical instead of a talk show. What is it?"

"WCRB. Pretty much the only station I listen to when I drive."

As we turned onto the dirt road that led to the barn, Bach's "Goldberg Variations" began playing. The tinny notes of the harpsichord distracted me from the rattle of my car on the rutted road. When I pulled in front of the barn, it hit me. I turned the car off and said. "*Er war Gift.*"

"What are you talking about?" said Rachel as she unbuckled her seat belt.

"The German couple we passed when we came out of Clive's, the German composer. I just made the connection."

"To show off your German? I don't get it."

"Remember in American Studies when Lucille would tell us that German was almost declared the official language of the United States, and would show off by tossing out a bunch of German phrases."

"German coming close to being our official language is an urban myth."

"I know. I took four years of German at UNH. *Er war Gift. Gift* in German means *poison. Now* I think Lucille was saying that Joseph was poison to her."

"Maybe that's why Joseph didn't like her."

"And maybe it explains something about his death."

We stepped out of the car into the cold air with our private thoughts of what Lucille meant by using the German word for *poison.* If she meant the allusion at all.

5

Rachel and I took hold of the door handle the way we did that bright September noon nearly thirty years ago. Inside was small, maybe twelve hundred square feet, a farmer's barn, not a dairy barn. Our headlamps cast a stream of light onto Teddy's tractor that was parked just inside the door. An owl swooped from the rafters into a stall, then flew back with some kind of prey in its beak. I almost tripped over two fuel containers when I walked around the tractor. Wherever I shined my headlamp, I saw farm equipment or cans with drips of green paint left from the painting Teddy did in the fall on the cabins where he housed his Jamaican workers. A door that looked like it belonged inside one of the cabins rested on a pile of sawdust next to a table saw. Unlike Seth Thompson, Teddy cared about his workers and kept their cabins in good repair.

At the far end of the barn, the ladder into the loft was only a shadow. Another shadow lay beneath the loft in what should have been empty space. It was too large to be a dead animal and there was no rotting smell.

I reached for Rachel's hand, my own pulsing beneath my glove. We moved closer. "It looks like a shrine," I whispered as if I were trying not to disturb whatever ghosts lurked in the stalls where the cows had been before whatever health-obsessed agency evicted them.

We stood together looking down. Clean hay had been spread onto the dirt floor to make a bed. Or a grave. The fresh bale was placed in front of it as a kind of chair. At the foot of the hay bed, a fat candle in a solid brass holder was burned halfway down, a charcoal drawing resting beside it. Rachel picked up the drawing, holding it so we could both see by the light of our headlamps. It was a likeness of Joseph, his hair curled along his forehead, his eyes large, a dimple next to his wide smile. The head floated bodiless on the white sheet of paper.

Rachel handed the drawing to me. "The strokes aren't angry. Someone was lighting a candle, sitting on the hay bale and remembering him."

"Maybe Teddy. Or maybe his killer is still alive and feeling guilty."

Rachel took the drawing back and placed it on the floor. "I asked Teddy yesterday if teenagers still used the barn."

"They do. I sometimes hear them talking at youth group. I wonder why Teddy doesn't get a lock."

"I asked him the same thing. He said he'd need to attach a hinge to the door frame and use a chain and padlock. Kids would break it and the frame would splinter. Elizabeth said the worst they do is leave beer cans around. I'm afraid she's been hanging out here."

Rachel was right. Elizabeth was a lot like us in high school. She was quirky, but she wasn't rebellious. She often reminded me of Rachel, smart, talented, honest in a way some people read as opinionated. "Could she have left this drawing? Trying to connect with the boy who was her father's best friend?"

"She's seen photos of Joseph."

I bent down to touch the candle. "One spark and this place would go up in flames. We should call the police."

"Why? They're useless. If they weren't, they would have found Joseph's killer in 1990."

"We should at least tell Teddy."

45

Rachel stepped away from the shrine or whatever it was. "In the morning. Right now I'm going to the loft. You should look in all the stalls."

"For what?"

"Something round and hard." She walked past the bed of hay, careful not to disturb it, and climbed a ladder rickety from age and disrepair.

I wouldn't find anything in the stalls. Unless there was something that would tell me who left the drawing of Joseph. They were simple rectangular spaces separated by four-foot-high wooden barriers, some of them fallen onto the dirt. Teddy had removed the slatted gates and used the stalls for hay that he let rot to sell for mulch. Once when I was buying a bale, he explained the difference in size. The larger one was a stall for birthing, the smaller for the calf. The other four were all about ten by twelve feet and opened to a trench in the back for manure. The few years Seth kept cows, he used a wooden stanchion in the middle of the barn to milk his cows. During the day, he would lead them together to the pasture across the street. Every other stall had a window above it. They were dirty enough that even in daytime almost no light would shine in.

In the stall closest to the shrine, the wheelbarrow Joseph must have fallen against was turned upside down on dirt that was hardened to ice in the cold. I touched the handle and spoke in a whisper, "Joseph, we'll find your killer." I backed out of the stall and worked my way through the others. All but one was empty of hay. A dead mouse lay in the corner of the calf stall, maggots finishing what little its killer left behind. Shivering, I thought of Joseph and a passage from Job. "They lie down in the dust, and the worms cover them." At the largest stall near the door, I jumped, a startled cry escaping me.

Rachel called down from the loft. "Did you find something?"

"A raccoon."

"At least it's not a skunk. I'm coming down."

The raccoon looked at me with its bandit eyes, hissed, then walked slowly to the barn door. He left three well-formed droppings on the remnants of mulch hay. A car passed by, illuminating the animal. I stepped away from the door. Moments later the car turned around and passed again, heading back to town.

Rachel came up beside me. "Do you think whoever just drove by saw us?"

I let out the breath I'd been holding. "My car's a dark color, so I don't think so. But we'd better get out of here soon."

I looked away from the door toward the corner at the end of the barn. In the open space behind the last stall, I could just make out a wrought iron ring.

Rachel saw what I was looking at. Without speaking, she walked to what was a trap door and knelt to pull on the iron ring. Her headlamp flickered and went out. "Shit." She stood and moved closer to my light. Her headlamp caught in her hair when she tried to take it off. I helped her untangle it, shook it, turned it off and on again. Nothing.

"We need to see what's under that trap door." She took the headlamp from me and repeated my movements. "Shit."

"Exactly what's down there."

"What's that mean?"

"Manure. These old barns have manure holes. Farmers raked the manure out of the trenches behind the stalls and into the hole. There should be a door outside that Seth could open to get the manure for his fields."

"How do you know all this?"

"Teddy gave me a tour once when I was buying mulch hay for my tomatoes."

"Spare me the details. Just go down there and look." Rachel bent to pull on the iron ring.

I turned away so she lost the light of my headlamp. She often led me in high school, but she wasn't going to lead me into a manure hole in the dark.

She straightened herself. "Please, Deb, I need your light."

"I've already faced a maggot-covered rat and a raccoon. No way I'm going down there now."

A noise drew our eyes to the tractor and the outline of a long, low animal. It's beady eyes looked at me. "A fisher cat. Maybe they do live here. They're nasty."

Its scream penetrated my whole body like a cry of pain. Rachel was right that the barn held ghosts. Everything felt violent.

"Tomorrow, then," she said. "I'll get a new headlamp and go down myself."

I picked up the candle and the drawing. If they were meant as a shrine, it wasn't a shrine to a peaceful death.

Rachel's voice floated disembodied from the corner. "Leave them."

"Not the candle. It could start a fire."

"So could a match. Leave it. We'll come back." She walked to the door and I followed. We locked hands to roll it closed. The narrow light of my headlamp guided us past the rustlings we heard all around us.

I slowed at the barn after I dropped Rachel back at Teddy's. I pictured the hay bale. It was fresh, the drawing done by someone good enough to capture Joseph's likeness. Rachel? She was hiding something. She knew how to draw. She had loved Joseph in whatever fashion teenagers love. She could have come back to honor him as much as to mourn Mary. But when could she have done it? More likely Teddy or Elizabeth. The whole family was artistic. Even Janet. Maybe I was wrong and what we saw was a warning, not a shrine.

The rumor mill would have spread far enough that half the town would know we were searching for Joseph's killer. Anyone could figure out that we would visit the barn.

I turned on my radio to calm my imagination that had gone into overdrive. The strains of "Rhapsody in Blue" accompanied me to what passed for my driveway. By Monday, the driveway and my car would be buried under snow. When I opened the storm door, a folded piece of paper fell onto my too-thin boots where some hay had caught on the eyelet. If I'd known we were going to stop at the barn, I would have worn my hiking boots and heavy socks. My feet were freezing, and under my corduroy pants my legs weren't much warmer. I kept my glove on to pick up the paper. It looked like the same kind we found in the barn. Inside the kitchen, I put it still folded on the table, afraid to look, afraid it might be another drawing of Joseph.

I took off my gloves and hat, put them on the table next to the paper, and hung my parka on a chair. If I turned the paper over and saw another drawing of Joseph, it wouldn't have come from Rachel. She'd been with Teddy or me all day.

From the living room, my cuckoo clock sang out ten o'clock. When it finished, the house was silent. No wind rattled the storm windows. The furnace hadn't kicked on. I reached for the paper. It sounded loud against the table when I pulled it toward me. I unfolded it just as the furnace started. My words sounded with the furnace. "You idiot." The paper showed a drawing, poorly done, of a shovel. Under it was printed in block letters. "Will shovel snow. Call Andy Carkin. 673-7087." My neighbor. He was somewhere around eleven years old and as scrawny as weed. I'd call him in the morning. If the snow was as deep as predicted, I'd have to watch that he didn't get lost in a snowdrift. I left the paper on the table and went into the living room to check on the progress of the storm.

The fire in the woodstove was dead. I piled kindling and three logs in the stove and stuffed newspaper underneath them. The furnace was still rattling. If my feet ever thawed out, I'd be warm enough to sleep, so I'd wait until morning to light the fire. I turned on the television. The storm was building momentum. It would likely hit by Sunday afternoon and last for twenty-four hours. Monday's commute would be a mess. I'd heard enough and clicked off the weather.

On the table next to my bookcase, I noticed my landline blinking. I was tempted to ignore it, too exhausted to listen to messages. I unlaced my useless fashion boots and left them in front of the stove. They'd warm up in the morning after I lit the fire. The floor felt cold under my cotton socks. The phone kept blinking at me until I picked it up and heard, "You have three new messages."

The first one was from Lucille Larcom, telling me about choir practice for tomorrow's memorial service. The hired accompanist wasn't as good as Mary, but the practice went okay. I deleted the call and listened to the second one. Seth Thompson telling me he'd gone back to the library after dinner to get his hat. It was unlocked. He thought someone had been in my office. The papers on my desk weren't stacked the way they usually were and my paperweight wasn't on top of them. Seth knew my habits, but he could just be paranoid. It wouldn't be the first time he'd forgotten to lock the door. I deleted his message.

The last one started in silence. I was ready to delete it when a muffled voice said, "Forget Joseph." Nothing else. It sounded so electronic I couldn't tell if the voice was male or female. But I could tell that it was a threat.

I saved the message and double-checked the locks on my doors before I went upstairs for a bath. My clawfoot tub was a refuge for me nearly every night. Deep and cocooning with warm water to help me relax. Usually while I soaked, I'd read a *New York Times Book Review* to see what I might want to order for the library. Tonight,

I just lay in the tub, listening hard for any noise outside. When I got out and into my pajamas, I found Beethoven curled on my bed. Not a guard dog, but he'd comfort me. Putting on socks, I climbed into bed and rolled onto my stomach. Beethoven purred at my feet. I wanted to gather him in my arms and let him sleep against my chest to calm the pounding of my heart. If I tried to move him, he'd jump off the bed and find his way to his chair in the living room.

I pulled the covers over my head. Outside the air remained calm, masking the storm to come. An owl whoo'd in front of my window from the tree he called home. An image of an owl swooping down to feast on the rat in the barn pursued me into sleep.

6

A N ARRANGEMENT OF hothouse lilies carried no smell into the sanctuary. I walked up the aisle to a second row pew behind Rachel and Teddy, Janet and Elizabeth. They all looked to the center of the church at a photo of Mary on the side of the table opposite the flowers. She was sitting at the church organ, her face in profile, her head tipped upward the way she held it when the music moved her. Between the photo and the flowers, her ashes rested in the pottery urn, plain and earth-colored. Beneath the lid, I pictured the wedding ring that Pastor Pam buried with Mary's ashes. Ashes, photo, flowers. Who would take them after the service?

When Cathy and Nathan died, I refused a church funeral. Instead, we held a memorial service at the edge of the Atlantic ocean. The music came from a trumpet played by Nathan's brother, the mournful notes of "Taps" accompanied by the sound of the waves breaking on rocks. My husband's and my child's ashes, mingled together in one urn, rested on the table beside my bed. Every morning when I woke and every night when I climbed into bed, I spoke to them about my day or my dreams.

Last night and this morning, I told them what I hadn't told them in life. About why I wanted to go into Seth Thompson's barn that September day. I'd never confessed to Rachel. Perhaps now I would.

Lucille Larcom gave the first reading, "To every thing there is a season," from Ecclesiastes. Finished, she waited several seconds, studying the right side of the sanctuary before she returned to the choir, her face looking flushed in anger or embarrassment and accenting the red highlights in her hair.

While the choir rose and sang "Will the Circle Be Unbroken," I scanned the opposite side of the church for what Lucille saw. Conrad Donaldson, alone, three pews back. Lucille never talked about her ex father-in-law or about her brief marriage to Eric. Conrad had severed all his connections to Shelby after Lucille and Eric divorced. He would be almost seventy years old now. I could see that he'd aged well. His hair was salted gray but still thick. He had traded his aviator glasses for fashionable ones with black plastic frames. Someone told me he was retired and living alone on Lake Kanasatka in Moultonborough. Who told him about Mary's death? Why? He hadn't seen her for over twenty years.

After a prayer and another hymn, Teddy approached the pulpit to read from the Twenty-third Psalm. He unwrapped his arm from Rachel, who sat next to him in the pew in front of me. He paused at the communion table to look at the photo of Mary before he ascended the steps to the pulpit. He surprised me by addressing the congregation. Teddy was introverted, more at home in his vegetable fields than with people who frequented his farm stand. His voice was controlled as he spoke. "The Mary Wheeler I remember is the mother figure who helped my sister Rachel and me through our school years after our own mother died. She swam with us, she hiked with us, she taught us piano. She fed us and made sure that our refrigerator was stocked with food alongside the beer our father drank too much of. Often we called her Mum. I thought of Joseph as my brother." He looked at Rachel. "My sister… " He stopped and addressed the urn in the whispered tones I used when I talked to Cathy and Nathan. "Mum, thank you." I hadn't seen Teddy so emotional since the day Rachel and I told him that we found Joseph dead in the barn.

When it was my turn to deliver the eulogy, I had to steady myself with deep breaths before I began. "Mary Josephine Monroe, born September 12, 1952, in Concord, New Hampshire. Our Mary Wheeler. Whether in the old high school, or the new one we built in what was once a corn field, you knew her as the teacher who brought joy into her music classes. Perhaps you learned from her how to play the piano. Close your eyes and see Mary as you most remember her."

After allowing mourners a minute of silence, I spoke with my eyes closed. "I see Mary's strong hands and arms, toned from so many years of playing music. As most of you know, she lived across the street from me. I can still hear the notes of Chopin drifting through her window in the summer. She was a fine enough pianist that she could have pursued a professional career."

I opened my eyes, blinking away the tears that threatened to fall on my paper. "Perhaps you saw Mary paddling her kayak alone on Shelby Lake. Or saw her swimming, her legs as powerful at sixty-eight as they were when she was only thirty. How did she get to Shelby, our Mary? Why, if she wasn't teaching, did she spend so much time alone?

"There's no mystery to the past that brought her to us. She married Robert Wheeler when she was twenty-one. Six months later Robert was killed in Vietnam. Had Mary told him she was pregnant? I don't know. But I knew the child she bore and raised here in Shelby. Joseph Wheeler. We were classmates. Shelby High School, class of 1991. Joseph never graduated. He died at the beginning of his senior year. Her husband dead. Her only son dead. Mary could have given up on life. But she didn't. She became the Mary we often saw alone, but who we more often played music with or laughed with at our summer fair or our high school graduations."

I continued with a few of my strongest memories without

mentioning that Mary had been my model for how to survive the death of a husband and child. I finished without breaking down, then asked anyone in the congregation who wanted to come to the pulpit to share a memory. Lucille came first, her face now as pale as her white choir robe. "I was only twenty-two when I first came to teach in Shelby. Mary mentored me. I had coffee with her after school the day she died. At sixty-eight, she was as enthusiastic about teaching as she had been in 1989. We talked about her plans to retire at the end of the year. She wanted to finish, still in love with teaching. She and her son Joseph were gifts to me as I learned to navigate the culture of Shelby High School."

That word again. A gift... or a poison?

Lucille went on a little too long in a shrill voice that shared memories more about herself than Mary. "Mary's future in retirement would have been as bright as the future Joseph was denied by whoever killed him." I recoiled at her last words. Were they aimed at Rachel and me, a denial of her own involvement?

Whispers sounded through the congregation until someone else rose to pay tribute to Mary. A half-a-dozen people spoke, all echoing each other. Finally, we stood for the closing hymn, "Let There Be Peace on Earth." *And* in Shelby, I thought.

Downstairs at the luncheon of hot soups and breads, I joined Rachel and Teddy and Janet. Elizabeth stood with her high school friends in the line for food. Teddy gripped my hands with both of his, so tight it hurt. "I thought I was over it, but it all came back."

Rachel took one of his hands. "I've never gotten over it. I loved Joseph."

Teddy shook off her hand and released mine. "I was talking about Mary and how she looked out for us when Mum died and Dad coped with the bottle. This was *her* funeral, not Joseph's. Damn

Lucille Larcom. Now I have to explain to Elizabeth how he died."

Janet moved beside him. "I'll explain to her before you get home in the truck. It'll make it easier." She took his hand in her comforting way and led him to the food table.

Rachel lingered. "She's good for him. Keeps reminding him that Mary's why he became the man he is. I like her."

"It hasn't been easy for her coming into this town with people like Seth Thompson here. She's a strong woman and they've raised a wonderful child. I don't think Elizabeth left that candle and drawing in the barn."

"Teddy's so stressed he's rattling like a piece of tin."

"We're all stressed."

"Drive back with him in his truck and calm him down."

"I'll go with Janet and Elizabeth. I make Teddy nervous."

Rachel left me alone and waiting for Bertha Whetmore to finish writing a condolence no relative would read. Bertha was so shrunken with age that I could read most of the entries over her shoulder, but I needed to be closer to decipher her wobbly handwriting. When she finished, she handed me the pen and pointed to a framed photo of Mary, Joseph, Conrad Donaldson and his son Eric. "I remember that boy of Mary's. Same name as my boy. Last I saw of my Joseph, he was just about that age."

I was too young to remember Joseph Whetmore, but I knew the story of how he snuck out of the house at dawn when he was seventeen. Seth Thompson drove him to the bus station in Nashua. He swore that the boy was going to Boston for a college interview. Whether Joseph ever contacted his mother again, I didn't know.

Bertha shuffled to the food table, leaving me to sign the guest book. I managed to read what she had written. "He murdered both of you. Bertha Whetmore."

Bertha was often confused. Was she thinking about her Joseph and Mary's? I had never heard that her son had been murdered.

Who was the "he" she referred to? I needed to find Bertha in one of her lucid moments and ask what she meant. First, I wrote a simple note in the book no one would read. "Mary. Neighbor. Mentor. Friend. I miss you, Deborah Strong."

I studied the photo next to the guest book. It wasn't one Lucille and I found. Conrad had his arm around Mary. They were both smiling. Joseph and Eric looked more angry than happy. It was summer in front of Mary's garden. Retouched, the white of her shasta daisies and the gold with reddish-brown centers of her gloriosa daisies could have been used for an advertisement in a seed catalogue. Who was the invisible photographer and who had put the photo on the table?

"She was beautiful," said a voice behind me.

"Mr. Donaldson."

"Conrad. No need for the 'Mr.' I recognized you right away. Rachel, too. Can't miss that long dark hair and bangs to her eyebrows. And Teddy. Both so thin that together they wouldn't be able to hold down a helium balloon."

"Mary was like a mother to them. I didn't know you were close to her."

"Mary was a good colleague and a friend."

I pointed to the photo of him and Mary and the two boys. "Did you bring this photo?"

"Faded, like my memory. It was nice to see you." He left, ignoring my question. He passed Lucille without speaking to her and barely nodded at Teddy.

Lucille watched him, her face a scowl. It looked like she raised her middle finger when he disappeared through the door. She joined me at the table. "What were you two talking about?"

I picked up the photo. "This. Do you know who put it here?"

"Must have been Conrad. He and Mary were having an affair." Her shrill voice carried through the room. Other voices stopped for a second then went back to their droning.

I almost dropped the photo. Joseph and Eric had kept their secret well. "Mary and Conrad look happy."

"They were."

"The boys don't."

"I don't know how they felt. I only know that when Joseph died, Mary broke off the relationship, and Conrad took that job at the New Hampshire Historical Society."

"Do you know who took the photo?"

"I don't." Lucille left me standing alone, wondering what else Joseph and Eric might have been hiding.

I found my way to the food table for a bowl of something that I'd force myself to eat. I scanned the room to find Bertha. She was seated on a chair eating stew and dripping much of it onto her sweater. A group of women almost as old as she surrounded her. I'd have to wait to ask her about what she wrote in the guest book.

Rachel came up beside me. "Is it good?"

"I suppose so. I don't know why people always eat after funerals. Listen to them." The room was peppered with the same kinds of laughter that followed most funeral services. After the solemnity of the service and the burial, people relaxed and shared funny stories. No laughter had followed Joseph's service. After his burial, Rachel and I had huddled with the group of high school kids who came back to the church for a reception. Balancing plates of sandwiches, we speculated about who could have killed him. When my parents came to tell me it was time to leave, my plate was still full, my throat too tight to swallow anything. From somewhere buried deep in my memory, I saw Mary sitting under an open window, accepting condolences. A figure stood outside the window looking in. The memory disappeared as quickly as it appeared, the figure never taking shape as male or female.

"People laugh because the person's death doesn't really affect them unless they were a relative," said Rachel.

"Or a lover. Did you know that Mary and Conrad Donaldson were having an affair?"

"Joseph told me. He didn't like it." I wondered what other secrets Rachel was keeping. I waited for her to say more, but she only said, "Janet's waiting. I have to leave. I'll pack to stay overnight. Pick me up around three."

When his family had left, Teddy found me and asked if I wanted a ride. I could see anger in his quick steps. Or sorrow. I had my car, but I walked him to his truck. "We all loved Mary," I said.

"Joseph, too." He slammed the door. As he drove away, I saw several pieces of hay caught at the back of the truck's bed. Had he created the shrine to Joseph? Or had Elizabeth created the drawing from a photo she'd seen of her father's high school friend?

When I went inside, Bertha was still sitting in a circle, the oldest of the old ladies. "Here, let me take that," I said as I reached for the bowl in her lap. It was scraped empty. She might be frail, but she still had an appetite. I carried the bowl into the kitchen where the Kindness Krew were washing dishes and preparing containers of leftovers. Funerals generated enough food to serve the dead as well as the living.

I accepted a container of leftover stew and carried it to Bertha. "I have leftovers for you. How about I drive you home?" More than helping her, I wanted to ask what she meant by writing "He murdered both of you." I wasn't as kind as the people working in the kitchen.

Bertha looked at the four women surrounding her. "Will that be okay?"

They nodded in such unison I couldn't tell who had been the driver. Bertha fumbled on the floor for the enormous pocketbook she'd been carrying since I was in high school. It was outdated even then, heavy black leather with a handle instead of a shoulder strap.

She put her arms into the coat she had draped over her shoulders and rose from a chair that had no arms for her to push on. She rested her pocketbook on the chair then buttoned her coat. It was the same one she wore when she came to the library on Tuesdays, thirty years old probably, but classic enough that it didn't look too much out of style. I stopped myself from taking her arm so she wouldn't fall. Bertha hated being treated like the old woman she was.

I held the door open for her, being sure to stand close enough that if she listed, I could catch her. When we reached my car, I settled her into my front seat and put the container of stew on her lap.

"It's nice and warm," she said. "They all loved Joseph."

"Mary's son," I said as I closed her door and got into the driver's side.

"They loved my Joseph." Her voice rasped with age. The stale smell of her ancient body mingled with the odor of the stew.

Bertha stayed quiet while I drove her home. Her house was several miles out of town on the dump road, close enough that she walked to town and the library until she was well into her eighties. The house was a relic, as old as the relics people discarded in the dump's recycle hut. The road was now developed with a dozen houses on a cul de sac behind hers. I preferred the relic to Irwin Trombly's cookie cutter house that was the closest to Bertha's. Maybe it was his house that had made me avoid a relationship with him.

I parked in the driveway, wondering who would shovel it so Bertha could at least get to the mailbox she had once painted with a design of leaves and a cardinal. Rachel and I used to imitate the whistle of a cardinal when we rode by on our bikes. We didn't mean to be cruel any more than when we chanted "to the dump, to the dump, to the dump, dump, dump" to the tune of the "William Tell Overture."

Bertha opened her door before I turned off the car engine. "Wait," I said. "I'll get that container of stew." I knew better than to say, "I'll help you." She was proud and accepted "kindnesses," but never "help." I took the container from her lap and waited for her to step out of the car. She bent to get her pocketbook, her black coat making her look like a child's stuffed bear. I walked close to her, fearing how long we'd have to stand in the cold while she searched for her house key.

"Never lock my door," she said as she turned the knob. "Got nothing to steal."

Until I'd gotten the "Forget Joseph" phone message, I never locked mine either.

After the cold outside, Bertha's house felt like she had the heat cranked to eighty degrees. I opened her refrigerator and set the stew next to a half-covered casserole of what looked like tuna and noodles. The shelves held milk, prune juice, oranges and apples, cheese and bologna. The top shelf was filled with bottles of Ensure. Bertha's diet might be dull, but she wouldn't starve.

"Take off your coat. Sit awhile." She peered at me through glasses fogged by the sudden change from cold to hot. She could have been imitating John Lennon if her granny glasses had been a little smaller. Without wiping them off, she walked into the hallway that separated the kitchen and living room. It led to a windowless front door made of oak as old as the house. I stood behind her, watching her struggle to hang her coat in the mothball odor of a tiny closet.

I followed her into the living room, which wasn't as dark as the hallway, but with its low ceilings and heavily curtained windows, was still dim. Bertha turned on a brass floor lamp. Its rose-colored shade cast an eerie pink glow into the room.

I hadn't visited Bertha since last summer when I had brought her an overflow of green beans and zucchini from my garden. Caring for old people wasn't one of my stronger traits. I lacked the patience to slow down. Feeling guilty, I slipped off the tan coat I'd worn to the funeral, and sat on the loveseat she'd arranged so it faced a fireplace that was covered with a mesh screen. A bucket of ashes sat next to it. I could smell the damp ashes and feel a draft coming down the chimney. Bertha must keep her flue open. "Do you use your fireplace in this cold?"

"Not so much. Sucks up all the heat. I should get a woodstove."

"Be careful tomorrow if we lose power. Keep that screen on if you need to start a fire."

"Joseph used to build my fires. He was a good boy."

"You wrote about Joseph in Mary's guest book."

"Silly thing. Guest book at a funeral. The dead can't read." Bertha sat in the chair next to me, chuckling as if she had made a joke.

"The guest book's for the living, not the dead."

"Her boy's dead. Same as mine."

"'He murdered both of you.' What did you mean when you wrote that in the book?"

Bertha faced me. Her eyes looked vacant under glasses that were no longer fogged. "Can't write in a book. You'll have to pay for it. Library's strict about that."

"Not a library book. The guest book at Mary's funeral."

"Mary?" Bertha was slipping into one of her memory lapses. Or concealing something she knew.

"Mary Wheeler. We just came from her funeral."

She pulled down an afghan that hung on the back of her chair and wrapped it around her legs. "I remember now. Sometimes I forget when I get tired."

"Did you forget what you wrote? 'He murdered both of you.'"

"Someone killed her boy."

"And yours?"

"My Joseph went off to college. He was a good boy." Bertha used the words she always used about her son.

I tried again. "Who did you mean when you wrote 'he'?"

"Don't know why I'd write that. He. She. God. Whoever. The boys are dead."

"Your Joseph, too?"

"He was a good boy. Went off to college."

I wouldn't get anything more from her today, so I stood and put on my coat. I bent down and touched her gently on the shoulders. "I'll leave you to nap now."

"Thank you for coming."

"Have some of that stew later. Be careful if it snows tonight. Call someone if you lose power."

"Phone won't work, but people always check on me. That's a kindness." She closed her eyes. Her head fell toward her chest and her shoulders bent forward. I tucked the afghan more tightly around her. It looked as old as she. But clean. Like her living room and kitchen. She was right. People showed her kindness.

7

THE AIR HELD the dampness of the late Saturday afternoon, the thermometer telling me it was no longer too cold to snow. I could feel the fast-approaching storm in my bones. Already the wind was picking up and the first flakes of snow were landing on the large diesel tank Teddy kept at the side of the barn. By morning it would be covered. Rachel and I put our hands together on the handle to the barn door. It creaked on its rollers. A deep cold was trapped inside by the below-zero nights we'd had since Christmas. We walked around the tractor, careful this time not to trip on the smaller fuel containers Teddy kept inside. The light shining through the open door and dirty windows was so dim, we could just make out the shape of the hay bale at the end of the barn. We turned on our headlamps, Rachel's working now with the new batteries I had put in. Our beams shone like twins as we walked to the shrine.

Rachel grabbed my arm when we reached it. "It's gone."

The hay bed, the bale, the candle in its brass holder were all untouched. The drawing was gone. A few pieces of hay showed that someone had walked to the trap door. It had been opened and placed back so it wasn't fully closed.

Rachel whispered, though there was no one in the barn to hear us. "We have to look in the hole."

I tried to pull the door open. Whoever had closed it left it so crooked that it stuck. Rachel pushed me aside and tugged. It dislodged, throwing her backwards into my chest. We kept each other from falling. I rubbed my finger across my nose at the musty odor surrounding us. "At least it doesn't smell like manure."

Rachel shone her light into the cellar. She no longer whispered. "Why would anyone want to go into a shit hole?"

"Maybe he had the weapon that killed Joseph. Wanted to throw it into a place the police searched thirty years ago."

"Or *she*. Lucille could have killed Joseph."

"Bertha Whetmore wrote something strange in the guest book after the funeral. 'He murdered both of you.' We should forget Lucille."

Rachel lifted her head so her headlamp shone into my eyes. "Why would Bertha write that?"

"When she saw Joseph's picture, she thought of her son. His name was also Joseph."

"Was he murdered, too?"

"I only know that he ran away. Maybe she's been keeping a secret all this time about the man who killed Joseph."

"Our Joseph, you mean? Bertha probably doesn't know a male from a female. Probably never did. She was a stiff old lady even when we were kids." Rachel pointed her headlamp back into the manure hole.

"Not so stiff that she didn't get pregnant."

"Maybe she was raped."

Could that have been another cold case? Something from sixty years ago when Shelby would have one resident who doubled as a cop and a carpenter? A crime that would have been ignored? I hoped not. I wanted Bertha to have known love.

Rachel lifted her head again. "Forget Bertha. She didn't take my drawing or throw it into the shit hole."

"My?"

"First we go down. Then I'll explain." Rachel jumped the four feet into the hole. I followed. It was small, maybe four feet square, just big enough to hold the manure that four or five cows would have produced. We couldn't stand up straight until we moved directly under the trap door, our bodies touching. The wind blew against the outer wall of the hole, and the manure that had long ago turned into dirt held a skim of ice. The space was covered in spider webs that we brushed away from our faces.

Rachel bent to pick up her drawing, folded like a paper airplane. It looked more like a white skate stuck against the lumpy surface. When she stood, she hit her head on the roof of the hole. "Shit." She moved under the trap door again so she could stand up straight.

"No shit now." I tried to dig a boot into the surface. It was frozen solid. Through air holes on the outside wall and cracks in the low door, I could just make out the frost-covered grass.

The hole itself was fully lighted from our headlamps. There was no ladder. We'd have to pull ourselves back into the barn. I wished whoever had thrown down the drawing had also thrown down the hay bale.

"I'm tall enough that I can make it out of this hole without a boost. You go first." Rachel crouched, wrapped her arms around the tops of my legs, and lifted. The barn smelled almost fresh after the hole. She handed me the airplaned paper. "Hold it until I get out." As she said, she was just taller enough than me to get the leverage she needed to pull herself up. She stood and brushed the spiders off her parka, then did the same to mine.

I clutched the drawing in my hand. "I'm waiting."

"Waiting for what?"

"An explanation. You said '*my* drawing.'"

"I drew it at Teddy's when I was awake the other night, staring at a photo of him and Joseph that he has on his bookcase. It calmed me down."

"Awake what night? I thought you arrived on Friday."

"I arrived Wednesday late."

"And waited until Friday to see me?" Rachel touched my face with her gloved hand. It felt as cold as she looked.

"I wasn't ready."

"Not ready to see the person who was your best friend?"

She stepped closer to me. "I'm sorry. It was stupid."

I backed away. The same feeling I'd had for two days gnawed at my frozen bones. She was hiding something. "Why bring all this to the barn? And how'd you get this hay bale here?"

"I didn't plan to. Teddy needed to get Elizabeth from basketball practice. Or was it volleyball or some club meeting?"

"Why didn't Janet get her?"

"He asked her to pick up some chicken feed when she finished showing a friend something about quilting. I volunteered to get the feed. When I went to the room I'm sharing with Elizabeth, I realized she could see the drawing on the table next to the bed I was sleeping in. I picked it up and drove to the feed store."

I kicked against the hay bale. "And just happened to buy this hay."

"I saw candles in brass holders first. Beeswax. I think they were left over from a Christmas display. That's when I got an idea for a shrine. I bought a candle and a holder and some matches. One of the workers loaded the hay bale along with the chicken feed into the truck bed. I paid cash so Teddy wouldn't find out."

"And carried it by yourself when you got here." I stopped kicking when a clump of hay fell out of the bale that must have weighed close to a hundred pounds.

"I just pushed it around the tractor to the end of the barn. It wasn't hard. You're right. I set up the shrine."

"And lit a candle that could have set the whole barn on fire."

"Truthfully, I didn't think of that. But I was really careful."

"Why bring me here? Why not just leave it?"

She looked toward the loft as if she were speaking to the air. Her headlamp lit a stream of dust particles. "I need to tell you something."

My body thawed. At last I might hear what, besides Joseph's death, had interrupted our friendship so many years ago. "Why now? Why not last night?"

She moved her gaze from the loft to the row of cow stalls. The stream of dust followed it. "Too many creepy signs. A dead rat. A raccoon. A fisher cat. And my headlamp going out. I wanted you to come back with me. I planned to tell you after we went into the manure hole."

"Well, we've got another problem."

She reached down for the candle and brushed hay over the spot where it had been. "The rats can feed on the hay all winter. What problem?"

"Someone knew we were here. Unless you came back and tossed this in the hole."

Rachel sucked in her breath and faced me, her eyes glazed. "Last night. The car that turned around."

The car might have been a coincidence, but it frightened me. "Someone was following us."

"Who would know we're looking for Joseph's killer?"

"Everyone. Jody, the clerk who was in the library, heard us talking. By now, she's told half the town." I unfolded the drawing. The back side of the paper was blank. When I turned it over, I saw words scrawled across Joseph's face. I handed the paper to Rachel.

She read out loud, "Forget Joseph."

"That's the same message someone left on my phone."

She took the drawing from me, crumpled it up, and stuck it in her pocket. "Someone left you a message? Let me listen."

"Later. It's on my landline at home. What were you going to tell me?" Through the open barn door, I saw that it was snowing hard. We needed to leave before we got caught on an unplowed road.

Rachel looked down at the barn floor. I strained to hear what she said. "My dreams. My paintings."

"What about them?"

"It wasn't just images of the barn. There was Joseph. And a baby. I'd dream of the baby crying and wake up to find my pillow soaked in my own tears. I'd start a painting and find that a branch of a tree looked like a baby. A rock would hold an image of Joseph."

The wind blew through the barn door carrying with it the confession I guessed Rachel was about to make. "You know where the images come from."

"I was pregnant." She pulled off her gloves and reached for strands of hair that fell from under Elizabeth's knit hat. "We had sex that night before he died. It was the first time for both of us."

"Here? In the barn?"

"In the loft."

"That's why you went up there last night?"

"To remember. We were in love. We promised to stay together forever." She stopped twisting her hair and wrapped her arms around herself. "Joseph left something here. That's why he came back."

I wanted to tell her what Joseph was looking for but she needed to finish her story. "The baby?" I asked. Rachel hadn't been visibly pregnant our senior year.

She unwrapped her arms and started on her hair again. She spoke to the loft more than to me. "It was Halloween before I realized I was pregnant. I didn't know what to do, so I went to Mary. Asked her to help me find someone who'd do an abortion. She refused. Told me about her relationship with Conrad Donaldson and how she'd broken it off. She was afraid of another hurt if anything happened to him. But she said she'd go back to him. They'd raise my child. As if a baby could replace Joseph. As if children don't bring hurt."

The pain I had felt losing Cathy surged through me as vast as the barn's empty room. "Why didn't you tell me? I could have helped."

Rachel looked at me instead of the loft. "Like you had a list of abortionists."

"We could have figured something out."

"In the end, it didn't matter. I miscarried and went on with my life as if nothing happened."

"It must have been awful for you the entire year."

"It was. I thought I'd get over it if I could leave Shelby and all of New Hampshire behind me. But ghosts don't get buried. They rise again."

The wind was blowing snow through the barn door. Snow wouldn't bury the past. The storm was going to be as violent as Joseph's death. "Maybe finding Joseph's killer will help."

She reached into her pocket for the drawing. "'Forget Joseph.' I can't. I'm his murderer as much as whoever killed him in this barn."

"That's irrational. And you know it. Think for a minute. Who would have known he was in the barn?"

She hugged herself again. "Maybe Teddy or Eric."

I thought a minute about those days following Joseph's death. "Not Eric. He was with his father at some history conference in Boston. Remember when they got back and found out Joseph was dead? Eric thought it was his fault."

"It was partly Eric's fault. Joseph and Teddy had both planned to stay overnight with him while his father was away. They were going to order pizza, watch something on Mr. Donaldson's new VCR, and drink some of my dad's beer that Teddy was going to bring."

Rachel had never told me this backstory. I asked now. "Why didn't Teddy stay with Joseph?"

"When Joseph came to pick him up, I was home. Joseph said we could take the beer and go to the barn. Teddy said that was a ridiculous idea. It would be loaded with kids on a Friday night binge. Joseph said no one would be there. Seth Thompson had been kicking them out every weekend. Threatening them with the police. Teddy was annoyed at the whole mess up of plans, angry that Joseph was including me. He refused to come. He went to the soccer game under the lights in Milford instead."

"So he went to the game, and you and Joseph went to the barn. Seth never came by to check it?"

"We closed the door before we went to the loft. We didn't hear anything. Didn't even remember to take the beer."

Joseph hadn't suggested the barn so they could have sex. I knew why he wanted to go there, why he would have gone even if he and Teddy had partied at Eric's. "It's my fault, too. I—"

Rachel interrupted me. "I remember something else. We went to Skip's afterwards. We had won the soccer game, and half the school was there celebrating. Even some of the teachers. Joseph left me with Teddy. Asked him to take me home. He was going to leave the car at his house and take his bike to get something he left in the barn."

"Why his bike? Why not just drive back?"

"When I asked him that, he said he was low on gas. Teddy had offered to drive him, but he said no. I thought he just wanted to bike and think about us. Don't you remember how often he rode at night?"

I didn't, but what mattered was that Teddy knew where Joseph was going. "So Teddy knew he would be in the barn. Did Teddy go out after you got home?"

Rachel defended her brother. "He'd never have killed Joseph. They were friends."

"Someone else must have heard Joseph say he was going back to the barn. Who was near you?"

She stared at the snow blowing into the barn as if it could help her recover a memory. "A couple of teachers were there talking with Teddy and Paul Sanderson."

"Paul the Pole?"

"Tall Paul. Apparently he had beat the school record for most goals in a game. The teachers were congratulating him."

"Which teachers?"

Rachel still stared at the snow. "I remember. I thought maybe they were on a date. The German teacher. What was his name?"

"Mr. Nordquist. If all the boys had a crush on Lucille Larcom, all the girls had one on Mr. Nordquist. Who was he with?"

"Lucille Larcom."

"*Er war Gift.* Let's get out of here before the snow gets any deeper."

8

OUTSIDE THE BARN, snow was already blowing into drifts. We struggled to push the door closed, then brushed off my car. As we drove away from the barn and Rachel's confession, I could just make out the road through the blinding snow. When we reached the center of town, the car spun around on the slippery pavement in front of the church. I righted it and drove slowly up Spring Hill Road, hoping I wouldn't go off the edge into someone's yard.

We ran from the car to the house, blocking the needles of snow from our faces. This was a full-on blizzard, not Robert Frost's snowy evening. Inside, we brushed the snow from our jackets and left our boots on the mat next to the door. Rachel set the candle and holder she'd taken from the barn onto the kitchen table. We went into the living room where Beethoven was sleeping in his chair.

Rachel reached down to pet him. "You have a cat? I thought you didn't like animals."

"Beethoven was Mary's cat. I'm warming up to him." I reached for the two coat hangers that hung from hooks on a beam above my woodstove. Eight hooks had been there at least a hundred years, enough, I imagined, for the original owner's family. I was glad I kept two coat hangers on them even though I never had company in winter. We took off hats, gloves, scarves, and lay them on the stone hearth that surrounded the stove.

73

Rachel scanned the room. Two chairs, upholstered in a soft maroon, faced the stove. I'd arranged the matching sofa so I could look at the stove or the television. The bookshelves on the opposite wall were tightly packed.

"I'm surprised you have so many books," said Rachel.

"Even librarians want to own some." My shelves held mostly nineteenth-century novels, biographies of my favorite writers, and collections of poetry no one would check out if I purchased them for the library.

Rachel settled comfortably into one of the chairs. "I see that. Who's in the photos?"

"My ancestors. All from Shelby." On the tiny bit of wall space I had, I'd hung framed photos of my great-grandmother sitting on a rocking chair reading a book, my great-grandfather driving a cart behind a pony named Prince, my grandparents in front of their house in Shelby that had been lost to fire before I was born. Looking at the photos made me think of Mary and how she had no family. The cuckoo clock that hung on a narrow wall space between the hallway and the front door cried out six o'clock. It sounded like a death knell.

"Nice set-up," said Rachel.

"It's a lot of house for one person. Makes me feel guilty."

"Don't. We have enough other things to make us feel guilty."

"Guilt's not always rational. I'll get our boots, let them dry by the fire." I went into the kitchen, debating with myself whether I should tell Rachel tonight what I'd been able to tell no one except Charles Tibbetts when he was counseling me after Joseph's death. Not even Nathan.

When I carried the boots into the living room, I found Rachel raking the ashes to start the fire burning again.

"Makes me think of my dad. No matter how hung over he was, he always got up to keep our fire burning." She lay some kindling and a couple of logs onto the ashes. Before she crumpled newspapers to light under the kindling, she reached for her parka on the ancient hook. She pulled the drawing from its pocket, crumpled it with the newspaper, and used a poker to coax the papers under the kindling.

I handed her matches that I kept on the telephone table. The phone light wasn't blinking. Maybe defacing Rachel's drawing had been enough for whoever made that call.

Rachel lit the papers. She stayed kneeling until the fire roared to life, then closed the door to the stove. When she stood up, her face was pink from the flames. "I miss this."

"Really? I thought you hated snow and cold. That's why you went south for college."

"Partly that. Like I told you in the barn, I mostly needed to get away from remembering Joseph. And from my dad. His drinking got even worse after Joseph died."

"You left Teddy alone."

"Mary told me I should go. Teddy had just a year of high school left. He'd be okay. She told me she'd watch out for him."

"He turned out well. He's quiet, but he's a good farmer and a great father."

"I'm glad I came back, even though I make him nervous." She stepped away from the heat of the fire.

"You should visit more often."

"Maybe. Let me listen to the phone message."

I took the receiver off its cradle, handed it to her, then pressed the play button. I studied her face as she listened. Her furrowed brow swept her bangs along her eyebrows. "Can you tell if it's male or female?"

She listened again. "No. It sounds more like a machine than a voice." She handed the phone back to me. "Now what?"

I put the receiver on its cradle, trying to decide how to answer her. Through the window, I saw a car inching its way toward the center of town. Seth Thompson in his Jeep. Spring Hill Road was short, only about a quarter mile of residential houses and the ballpark. It connected to a state road that ran left into Massachusetts and right into Milford. Plows would be trying to keep up with the accumulating snow. Seth slowed almost to a stop as he passed between my house and Mary's. Bullets of snow hit his headlights as he continued on.

I turned away from the window. Rachel moved closer to the woodstove again, warming her back by the rekindled fire. "You've got some New Hampshire left in you."

"What's that mean?"

"Warming yourself at the stove. Why is it only women who do that?"

"Protection. Not just from the cold. From men who leave threatening messages." She rubbed the fire's warmth into her low back. "Unless Lucille left the message. Who just drove by?"

"Seth Thompson in his Jeep. Don't know why he'd be out in this storm, but then again, he's one of those guys who loves to confront the weather. No warming his considerable backside by the fire."

Rachel moved away from the stove to look out the window. "Confront the weather. I like that idea. Let's go outside and make snow angels."

"You're kidding."

"I haven't been in a snowstorm since I was eighteen years old. I'm not kidding." She reached for her jacket. "Please. Just for a few minutes."

"Backyard. It's more sheltered."

As we bundled up and went outside, I caught Rachel's enthusiasm. A maple tree, now barren of leaves, shaded my yard and Andy Carkin's house next door during the dog days of summer. My neighbors on the opposite side had moved in two years ago. The first thing they did was build a six-foot fence around their entire backyard. No one ever gathered there, but in the fall I suspected what I smelled was marijuana growing, not a skunk. On the rare occasions I saw them, we'd say hello, comment on the weather, and wish each other a good day. If I ever got sick, they wouldn't be the ones who brought the chicken soup. Tonight, I was glad for the fence that helped block the wind.

"Whooee!" Rachel twisted and let herself fall backwards into the virgin snow. I followed her, just far enough away that our arms and legs wouldn't touch when we flapped them to make angels. The snow was soft. The blizzard of flakes above us looked like a rapidly flowing stream. I understood how a person could lie down and let the snow become a shroud.

Rachel began to make half-circles with her arms and legs. I made mine, the downward swoop like a swimmer doing a back stroke. We stopped our motions and lay as stiff as Teddy the Tin Man.

Rachel's voice reached me through the streaming flakes. "How did we get up so we didn't ruin our angels?"

"Someone would lean over, take our hands, and pull us up."

"Joseph did that."

"So did lots of other people. Stay where you are. I'll pull you up." I did a move I'd perfected in pilates. Reached my arms to the sky and rolled up to a sitting position. I bent my knees and stood, my right hand touching the snow to give me a boost. I jumped away to see how much I'd disturbed my angel. Not bad. I left only a ball-shaped indentation where my legs had formed the gown.

I shook off the snow along with my image of a ball and moved in front of Rachel. She gave me her hands and I pulled. We stepped backwards away from our angels.

Rachel put her arm around me. "Do you ever wish we were kids again?"

"*Little* kids. Back when we believed the world was good."

"Back when I still had a mother. When I was lying in the snow, I thought about how death could actually be peaceful."

"So did I. But it's not peaceful now. This storm's getting violent. Let's get inside and out of these wet clothes. We need to make dinner before the power goes out."

"What will we make?"

"Pizza, like when we were kids."

An hour later, I'd given up my bath routine and we'd both showered, put on pajamas, and hung our wet clothes on a rack that we set up next to the woodstove. Rachel was spreading tomato sauce on the pizza dough I'd rolled out. She began arranging pepperoni and red and green peppers into a kaleidoscopic design. Not like thirty years ago when we slapped toppings on willy-nilly.

"You design pizza like an abstract painting," I said as I sprinkled on mozzarella.

"Pizza art to ward off my dreams of Joseph and a baby. I think I won't dream tonight."

I coaxed the pizza onto the stone I'd heated in the oven and set the timer. "Eighteen minutes. A glass of wine or a beer while it cooks?"

"Beer. Always beer with pizza."

I took two Smuttynose pale ales out of the refrigerator and we sat at the kitchen table to wait.

"Smuttynose," said Rachel. "Named after that island where two women were murdered?"

"Karen and Anethe Christensen. In 1873."

"Who did it?"

"I think Maren Hontvet, the only other woman on the island that night who wasn't murdered. But a fisherman named Louis Wagner was hanged for it."

"A female murderer. Like—"

"Don't say it." I grabbed my beer and gulped a first swallow.

Rachel raised her bottle and drank, long and deliberately. Finished, she rubbed the bottle between her hands. "Whoever thought up the name for the beer has a macabre sense of humor."

"And a nose for marketing."

"Maybe the police were wrong. Maybe it was a beer bottle, not something ball-shaped, that killed Joseph."

"If it was, we'll never find the weapon to tie to his killer." The neck of my beer felt like a weapon. I rested it back on the table and moved my hand lower.

"I shouldn't have burned that drawing. We could've compared handwriting. Don't erase the phone message. We can trace the call. You should have Caller ID."

"Anyone who wants to talk with me can leave a message."

"'Forget Joseph.'" Rachel drank again from her Smuttynose.

I sipped mine. "What do you propose we do? We have no convincing suspects."

"We do. Lucille. She wrote 'poison.'"

A gust of wind blew my storm door open so wide it hit the side of the house. I got up to latch it. When I opened the inside door, snow blew onto my bathrobe. I latched the storm door and brushed the snow off before I locked the interior door against the cold. "Maybe she really meant 'gift.' What would be her motive? And why would Bertha have written 'he'?"

"Bertha gets confused. Maybe Lucille was sleeping with Eric and Joseph knew it."

"And never told you."

"He was a good friend to Eric. He would have protected him. And Lucille knew Joseph was going back to the barn."

Before I could tell her why Joseph went back, the buzzer sounded to announce that our pizza was done. I took it out of the oven, moved it to a plate, then sliced it into eight pieces and set it on the table next to the salad we managed to put together with the romaine, apples, and walnuts that I kept on hand for winter salads.

I bit into my pizza. I should have waited for it to cool. The roof of my mouth would still feel burned in the morning.

Rachel took a few bites of salad before she tried her pizza. "We did good work. This is delicious." She stood up to get another beer from the refrigerator. When she sat down again, she said, "Seth Thompson could have done it."

"Why?"

"Angry that someone was in his barn again. Maybe he's not as harmless as you think. Before I go back to New Orleans, I will find out who killed Joseph."

I reached for another piece of pizza. Before I got it onto my plate, the lights flickered and went out. I felt my way to the window. Without lights to highlight the snow, it fell almost invisible against the black sky. I used the kitchen counter to feel my way to my pie safe. Its four shelves, each intended for one pie, held a stack of assorted-sized pie plates I rarely used, a casserole dish, flashlights and batteries, and my collection of candles. I fumbled for a flashlight, my hand hitting one of our headlamps first. I turned it on, slipped it onto my head, and found the one Rachel had used.

"Too bright," said Rachel. "Don't you have candles?"

I kept the headlamp on and hung Rachel's over my arm while I found my set of brass candle holders. With my free hand, I picked up a box of matches and two hand-dipped candles attached together by their wicks and the glass drip catchers I'd slip over the tapers. The headlamp lighted my way to the table. The cuckoo clock cried out nine. We'd go to bed early tonight, bundle under blankets to stave off the cold that would invade the house all too soon.

I used the pizza cutter to separate the candles and a match to melt some wax into the holders so the candles wouldn't get knocked over. The drip catchers slipped easily over them. When I lit the wicks, they exploded in flame because I hadn't trimmed them low enough.

As I turned off my headlamp and the wicks lowered, Rachel's face glowed on the opposite side of the table. "I loved storms like this when my mother was alive. We'd play pioneers, wrap ourselves in blankets, and cook hotdogs in the fireplace."

"I like a fireplace better than a woodstove. More romantic. But when I bought this house, the woodstove was more efficient. I inserted it into the fireplace, and now I content myself by opening its door."

"Has there been romance?"

"A few tries, but nothing's clicked. I can never get beyond remembering Nathan and Cathy."

"They're your ghosts the same as Joseph is mine."

Beethoven found his way into the kitchen and began crunching his dry cat food. "We should be like cats," I said. "Able to see in the dark."

"And able to use a litter box instead of a toilet we can't flush."

"You remember."

Rachel swallowed the last of her beer. "I shouldn't have had the second one. Extra pee in that unflushable toilet. How do you handle it? We used to fill the bathtub if a storm was coming and use a bucket of water from it to flush."

"When we finish our pizza, I'll show you. My dad always drove to the lake and filled containers. He hated to fill the tub and waste water if no storm came."

Newcomers to Shelby bought generators and lost the community spirit of making it through a storm. Occasionally, we'd be out of power for days or even a week. The fire department would switch on its generator, serve meals concocted from food donated by people who worried about it spoiling. Everyone in Shelby had a private well, and therefore, no water without a source of electricity, so the department opened a hose for filling water buckets. There was no talk about adding a town water or sewer system any more than there was of having trash pick-up.

We finished our pizza and carried our plates to the sink, careful not to turn on the water. Beethoven brushed against me as he squeezed through the crack in the door I left open so he could get into the cellar. I handed Rachel her headlamp. "We need better light for this. Come down cellar and we'll get my water supply."

We descended the steep stairs into a cellar that wasn't much better than the barn's manure hole. The walls were granite boulders, the floor, dirt. I'd been afraid Beethoven would prefer the dirt to his litter box, but he was used to his box and had already adapted. He was scratching the litter when we reached the cellar floor, jumped out of the box, and climbed back upstairs. In the summer, the cellar smelled of damp earth. Now it smelled of cat litter. Eventually, I'd buy some odor eater jars.

I pointed Rachel to the blue five-gallon jugs I kept filled. "One for the downstairs bathroom, one for upstairs. Careful, they're heavy."

With my free hand, I picked up my old Princess phone that I kept on a shelf in the cellar. It was held together with bright blue duct tape.

Rachel turned her headlamp so its light shone on it. "Is that the phone you had in high school?"

"The only one that works with the electricity out. In case someone calls my landline instead of my cell."

"You won't get messages on it."

I wanted no more 'Forget Joseph' messages. But if the cell towers went down, I wanted a way to communicate even though not many people in the outside world kept an old phone around.

We carried the water jugs upstairs, leaving one in the downstairs bathroom next to the kitchen. I carried the other to the upstairs bathroom, using both hands and a boost to the jug with my legs.

I came back downstairs empty handed. Rachel stood in front of the kitchen window looking at the backyard. "Our snow angels are already covered."

"We can make more tomorrow." Our thirty-year separation had faded when we were outside, and I felt as close to Rachel now as when we were kids. I opened the refrigerator and took out a gallon jug of water. "For brushing teeth. I'm glad we took showers when we came inside. It might be a few days before we get another."

"Your food will spoil."

"I'm afraid my refrigerator isn't well stocked. What little there is will keep overnight. In the morning, we'll pack a cooler and set it in the snow."

Rachel turned off her headlamp. "It's been a long day. I'm taking a candle and going to bed."

The day had been more emotional than long. I realized how tired I was. If I had been alone, I'd have collapsed in a chair by the woodstove and slept there until morning.

"We each get one toilet flush," I said. "Use the downstairs bathroom while I load wood into the stove. There should be enough ashes left in the morning to start another fire. It'll be cold, though."

I left my headlamp on the kitchen table and used a trickle of water from the kitchen sink to fill Beethoven's water bowl. I held the clean water jug in one hand and my candle in the other and went into the living room. Beethoven wasn't in his chair, so I knew he was hunkered down on my bed.

Rachel held the candle before her when she came into the living room. She reminded me of Lady Macbeth, and how I'd always been thankful that Joseph wasn't killed with a dagger. We climbed the stairs together. Rachel used the bathroom first to brush her teeth. When she was finished, I said, "Blow out the candle as soon as you get in bed."

"Of course. I'm not an idiot." She gave me a tentative hug, the closeness we had felt outside fading when she closed the door behind her.

I used my one flush, and water from the clean jug to brush my teeth. The candlelight softened the face I saw in the mirror. The same short hair with flipped bangs I'd had in high school, but flecked heavily with gray now. Even at forty-seven, Rachel was more glamorous than she'd been in high school. I turned away from the mirror. I wasn't glamorous, but I wasn't fixated on the past. The day had told me to stop envying Rachel.

I woke once in the night. The wind still blew, but quieter now. I heard the cry of an animal in pain outside. Something caught by a coyote, I thought, until I realized the cry was coming from Rachel in the spare bedroom.

9

THE SUN ROSE to a clear, still morning in the kind of brilliance that follows a storm. Snowbanks left by the town plow were still clean and the untraveled road was covered with a thin layer of fresh white.

Beethoven rubbed along my ankles as I rekindled the fire and ignored the burned feeling in my mouth from last night's pizza. In the kitchen, he jumped onto the counter to watch the nuthatches and chickadees at the feeder. The thermometer registered twenty-eight degrees. The sun would warm the air to the low thirties, so we'd have a day or two before the snow crusted over and the banks along the roads began to look like dirt piles.

I lifted Beethoven off the counter and filled his dish with dry food. While he ate, I went into the cellar for a cooler to load with perishables that I would set in the snow outside my kitchen door. As I cleaned Beethoven's litter box, shoveling the clumps into a bucket I kept covered, I pushed away the image of Seth Thompson's manure hole.

Rachel was standing at the kitchen window when I came up from the cellar. "God's in his Heaven/All's right with the world," I said.

"Isn't that something your mother used to say?"

"Always on a beautiful morning. It's a line from Robert Browning." In fact, it was the line she said before Rachel and I went off on our bicycles the day we found Joseph dead.

Rachel opened the refrigerator door. "Cold pizza for breakfast? We can split the one piece that's left. Chase it down with a glass of milk, unless you want to greet the morning with a beer."

I lifted a teapot off the stove. "We can do better. I filled the pot before the power went out. There's enough water for coffee and oatmeal. Gas stove and matches to light the burners. I'm a Girl Scout. 'Be prepared.'"

"Isn't that the Boy Scout motto?"

"Both I think. Actually, I have no idea. I never joined Girl Scouts."

"*We* never joined. Remember how on Girl Scout days we'd be the only girls who walked home instead of staying at school for the meetings?"

I lit the burners and measured water into the oatmeal. "I remember. We'd dump our backpacks at my house and head outside, no matter the weather."

"And spy on the boys at the camp they were building in the woods."

"Teddy, Eric, Joseph. A couple others I don't remember. Even in elementary school, you had a crush on Joseph." I started to unload the refrigerator food into the cooler, leaving milk on the counter. The container felt a little warm, but the milk would still be okay. There'd be just enough for our oatmeal.

"I dreamed about Joseph again last night. He kept reaching for a baby crying outside my window."

"You heard the shrieking of the wind outside the windows. There are no ghosts here."

"Just in the cobwebs of my head."

The teapot whistled over my thought that she was mentally ill. Or at least needed counseling. Her obsession had morphed into something more serious than twisting her hair. Before she went back to New Orleans, I'd suggest she find a professional to talk with. But not today, when we were just finding each other again.

"Oatmeal should be almost done. Stir it while I make the coffee." I measured coffee into a Melitta cone and slowly poured water over it. While it dripped, I picked up the cooler to set it outside. I used my whole body to open the door wide enough against the snowbank to fit the cooler. I wondered how we'd shovel ourselves out until I saw Andy Carkin walking up my driveway. He had just passed my car and I wanted to send out a toboggan to help him navigate the last few feet to my doorstep. The snow was up to his knees and he struggled with each step. He reached the door and said, "Can I shovel for you?"

"You sure can. Start here at the door. You can shovel your way out. Rachel and I will help as soon as we've finished breakfast."

"Rachel?"

"Ted Cummings' sister. She's visiting for a week."

Andy motioned toward Mary's house. "I liked Mrs. Wheeler. Think I should shovel her driveway?"

I started to say, "She'd like that," before I remembered that she was dead. "If you have energy left after mine."

"First, I have to do Miss Larcom's."

"Get to it then. We'll help in about a half hour."

When I closed the door, Rachel was shivering from the blast of cold air. "Oatmeal's ready. Can we eat in the living room? It's freezing in here."

"As close to the woodstove as we can get." I opened the cupboard for two bowls. We filled them with oatmeal. I cut up the lone banana that lay on the counter and stirred slices into our bowls, then topped everything with sugar I kept in a pottery jar on the counter. Rachel poured in the milk, down to the last drop. The bottom of the pan was covered in baked-on oatmeal, so I opened the door again and filled it with snow. When I had to face dirty dishes, the oatmeal would peel right off.

We carried our breakfasts into the living room where Beethoven had taken over one of the chairs by the stove. I nudged him away and watched him climb the stairs. He was welcome to my bed in my freezing room. We put our coffee cups on a barrel between the chairs that I used as a table.

Rachel settled herself into a chair. She tasted her oatmeal. "This is good. You know how to handle a storm." She lifted her cup from the barrel and sipped. "I like the barrel."

"Remember Bruce Tasker?"

"The school janitor we all liked?"

"Turns out he was also a talented woodworker. When he retired, he started to make these barrels. The old-fashioned way. Wooden staves bound with rings, lids that people can buy plain or cushioned with fabric. I have another one in my bedroom that I use to store my extra linens."

"I could use one in my studio. Fill it with my paint splattered clothes and drop cloths."

"You have a studio?"

"I call it that. It's just a shed in back of the house I bought after Hurricane Katrina knocked down real estate prices, along with half the structures in the city."

"Did you lose much of your art in the storm?"

"I had packed it all into my car when I drove to my friend's in Savannah. I lost easels and paints and my rental apartment. But I came out well. I used renter's insurance to collect for everything Katrina destroyed and then bought a house on higher ground."

"There's high ground in New Orleans?"

"Higher, not high. I cared about a lot of the things I lost, but in the long run, I'm better off. Except for the dreams. They started after Katrina."

"What happened after Katrina? That was a long time ago."

"At first it was just Joseph and the barn. A year ago, I bought a box like the one I lost in the storm. I'd look into its emptiness every day. That's when Joseph and the baby began to appear in my dreams and in my art."

"What was in the box you lost?"

She scraped the last of the oatmeal from her bowl as if she were scraping away memories. "His class ring, notes he wrote to me, a couple of badly written poems, some photographs. There was one thing I never understood. I found it in my locker after he died."

"You never told me you found something." I felt resentment rising at all the secrets Rachel had kept from me.

"A note. I didn't know what it meant. Still don't. It was just one line. 'Do you have my German book?' Why would I have his book? I never took German until college."

I finished the last of my coffee and oatmeal, and picked up a log to put on the fire. The fire crackled and gobbled the log I put in, igniting my fear.

"I wish the fire could burn away my guilt," said Rachel. "Joseph and I should never have gone to the barn."

I sat back in the chair, turning so I could face her and confess. "Burn away my guilt as well."

"That Nathan and Cathy died? That wasn't your fault."

"It's my fault that Joseph went to the barn."

Rachel stopped looking at the woodstove and faced me. "What do you mean?"

I breathed in the scent of burning, then let the air out of my lungs, and with it, the guilt I'd been carrying since Joseph died. "I took his book and hid it."

Rachel jumped from her chair and glared down on me. "Whatever for?"

"German class. Mr. Nordquist challenged us to a scavenger hunt. We had the week to find an object and hide it. We drew names and gave the person a clue in German. After school on that Friday,

Joseph left his book on his desk while he and Teddy went outside to play catch. I stuck it inside my jacket and told them I was going for a bike ride. I rode around for half an hour trying to think of a dry place to hide it."

"Didn't Joseph notice it was gone when you got back?"

"I didn't go back to school that day. But I saw him when I was on my way home. I gave him the clue so he could find his book."

"What was the clue?"

"It was obscure. He probably figured it out when you were in the barn. I'm not surprised you didn't see it. Seth still kept hay bales to sell for mulch, so I pulled some hay from one and buried the book under it in one of the stalls."

She grabbed my shirt and pulled me out of the chair. "You hid it in the barn?"

"There's something else."

"Isn't that enough? Joseph followed your clue, and that led him to his death."

Her fingers dug into my chest. I pushed her away. "Maybe I didn't want him to find the book. I wanted to be valedictorian. He had to study hard for German, and we were decimal points away from each other."

"So you sabotaged him."

"Not consciously. I made the clue too hard. *Deutsche Kühe springen nicht über den Mond. Sie gehen zum Heu.*"

"What does that mean?

"German cows don't jump over the moon. They head for the hay."

"You *bitch*. I shouldn't have come." Rachel tugged her parka off its hook, the hanger it was on landing hard on the stone hearth. Without tying the boots she stepped into, she ran to the kitchen. The door slammed before I had time to get my parka.

I jumped at the cuckoo clock ringing out my guilt while I tried to think of how to approach Rachel. I lifted down my parka and picked up the hat and scarf Elizabeth had made. In a kitchen drawer, I found two pairs of heavy mittens I used for shoveling and went outside. Rachel was standing in front of my car, her hands in her pockets, her body shaking. When I handed her the hat, scarf, and mittens, I saw what she was staring at.

Traced into the snow on my windshield were the words "Forget Joseph."

Rachel wrapped the scarf so tight around her neck it could have strangled her. Beneath her hat, her hair fell against it, shining in the sun. She began furiously brushing the snow off the windshield. She said out loud what I'd been telling myself for years. "He's dead because of you."

"I know. And now we have someone stalking us." I looked around the car for footprints, but they were obliterated by Andy Carkin who had worked his way to the snowbank the plow had left.

There was nothing more I could say. I'd confessed my guilt, lost my friendship, attracted a stalker. Numbed, I left Rachel to attack the snow on my car. I went into the cellar for a broom and a shovel. In the kitchen, I found my purse and took out a ten dollar bill. When I came back outside, Rachel was staring at Mary's house. She took the broom from me and used it like a weapon to brush the snow from the top of my car. It fell to the ground in clouds of light powder. I left her alone and walked to Andy. A plow had gone by when I was in the house, and he was throwing a shovelful of snow onto a mound as high as he was tall. If the snow in the road held any clue to who had written "Forget Joseph" on my windshield, it was buried in the snowbank now.

I helped him with the last of the snow, with each shovelful trying to throw away the past. When we finished, I managed to ask, "Did you see footprints when you came to my door?"

"They made a path for me." He thought a moment. "I guess they weren't yours. They stopped at your car."

"Were they a man's or a woman's?"

"Don't know. I was just glad they were there."

"It doesn't matter." My pounding heart quieted as I handed Andy the ten dollars. "Will this be enough for such a great job?"

He broke into a smile. "This is plenty, Mrs. Strong. Your friend is really pretty."

"She is."

"Miss Larcom's driveway is as long as yours. I'm not sure I'll have enough time to do Mrs. Wheeler's today. Do you think it can wait?"

"Get some rest after Miss Larcom's. There's no hurry on Mrs. Wheeler's walk, and there's no reason to do her driveway."

"Thanks again." Andy hoisted the shovel over his shoulder and headed down the street to Lucille's.

I walked toward Rachel, wondering what I'd be able to say to draw her back to me. She spoke first. "I want to make another snow angel."

I followed her into my backyard, hoping this was a first step toward forgiveness. The snow that had covered yesterday's angels glittered in the sun. We fell on our backs, flapping angel arms and legs. I closed my eyes and let the sun warm my face. It was my fault that Joseph went back to the barn. I rationalized that Joseph might have found the book earlier. Why else wouldn't he have looked for it with Rachel? I jumped up, ignoring my destroyed angel. "There's something else."

I pulled her up so her angel lay undisturbed. She looked calmer, the anger flashing from her eyes gone. Her voice was low and soft, no longer accusatory. "We're both at fault. If Joseph knew the book was in the barn, we should have looked for it instead of thinking only about sex."

"That's the thing. He must have gone back for the book. If the police had found it, they would have told me. I left a note inside. *Gutes Raten, mein Junge.*"

"Something *my boy*."

"*Good hunting, my boy*. I signed my name."

"What's the point?"

"Whoever killed Joseph must have that book."

10

WHEN WE CAME outside for the second time that morning, Seth Thompson was shoveling Mary's sidewalk. He threw the snow high enough in the air that it was hitting her bird feeder before it fell onto the five-foot mound he'd created. Birds flew around the feeder, as empty as Mary's house. A squirrel was burrowing under the snow looking for acorns it might have missed in the fall. Seth threw a shovelful of snow at him.

"Did he just target that squirrel?" said Rachel.

"He did. He hates squirrels from his days farming when they scavenged in his fields. I wonder why he's shoveling Mary's walk."

"We can ask." Rachel crossed the street that was still empty of cars.

Seth looked up when we reached him. He wore gloves and a heavy brown jacket, both soiled from years of work outside. He wore no hat, his shaggy hair falling over ears red from the cold. "Mornin'," he grunted, then went back to shoveling.

"Was it you who wrote in the snow on Deborah's car?" Rachel's obsession had only increased the boldness I remembered in her.

"Don't know what you're talking about." Seth lifted his shovel as if to throw snow in Rachel's face.

"It's nice of you to keep Mary's walk shoveled," I said, trying to stop a confrontation between them, though I knew something other than "nice" must have prompted Seth's shoveling.

He threw his shovelful toward the squirrel. "Gettin' paid. That lawyer of hers asked me. Pay's better than what you folks at the church and the library give me."

"Her lawyer?"

"Holly Hock. Stupid name. Sounds like a seed catalogue."

"It's Hoche."

"Still a stupid name."

I agreed with Seth, but I wouldn't admit it. I knew Holly and liked her. "Have you shoveled the ramp at the library?"

"Goin' there next." The bell for the ten o'clock church service rang through the still air. Seth looked toward the sound. "Church don't matter. Won't be a service today. That minister of yours asked me to post a sign on the door. Not that anyone will be dug out enough to get there, even if the heat was workin'."

Rachel touched my arm to signal she was ready to leave.

"It was quite a storm," I said, backing away from the next shovelful of snow Seth was about to unleash. "But it's a beautiful morning."

"Some folks like it." Seth threw the snow at the empty birdfeeder then scooped up another shovelful. I wondered what he'd aim at this time.

"He gives me the creeps," said Rachel as we made our way back to my driveway. "He was using that shovel like a weapon."

"Or like a pitchfork shoveling manure. I'm starting to agree with you. He could have killed Joseph."

Rachel quickened her steps. "One thing we know for sure is that Joseph wasn't killed with a shovel. We need to get into Seth's house. See if he has Joseph's German book. Or some kind of ball-like weapon."

"Seth's a recluse. We'll have to think up a good excuse."

At the house next to Lucille's, I waved at the two Phillips children who were rolling in the snow while their parents shoveled.

"Reminds me of us," said Rachel.

"They're sweet kids. They come to the library every Saturday and each one checks out half-a-dozen books. They'd take more, but the library limits them."

The children's yells followed us down the street to Lucille's house where Andy Carkin was shoveling her driveway. Rachel stopped in front of the house. "Should we knock on her door? Ask if she's okay in the storm? I could look around while you two talk."

"Talk about what?"

"I don't know. Mary's service. Her will. You'll think of something."

"If there is a will." Holly Hoche had hired Seth to shovel, so I knew there must be a will. But I didn't want to face Lucille and her shrill babbling about how well we'd planned Mary's service. "Later. Right now, we're going to the fire station. Find out what kind of damage the storm did, when we might get our power back."

A white cat ran into the road, barely visible against the snow, just as a car approached. The driver braked and skidded. He lowered his window. "You girls better get that cat home. I nearly ran into you when I braked." He drove on, hopefully into Massachusetts, identified by his license plate.

"I hate being called a girl," said Rachel.

"And I hate assumptions about who owns an animal."

When we reached the bottom of Spring Hill Road, Seth passed us, carrying his shovel over his shoulder. He walked straight into the center of town while we turned right toward the fire station. The road had been plowed and salted, and already the snowbanks were showing dirt. We passed Hank Huckabay's gas station. Like Seth Thompson, Hank was one of Shelby's old-timers who hated change. He'd lived in Shelby all his life and had owned the town's only gas station ever since I was a kid. There used to be a mound of old tires stacked behind it until the river flooded and washed them all downstream. I never learned what kind of cleanup he was forced to do, but I knew that he resented any environmental regulations the town put on him as an intrusion on his civil rights. Half-a-dozen junk Volkswagens had taken the place of his tires. Today, they looked like giant snow covered beetles. Once in a while someone would buy a stray part from Hank or ask to buy an entire car. Rumor said he wouldn't sell any of the Volkswagens because he wanted to keep the place an eyesore in the town he resented ever since it made him clean up the tires. As far as he was concerned, the idea of climate change was a hoax foisted on the country by Democrats.

Hank was pumping gas for Irwin Trombly, whose German Shepherd watched out the window of the front seat. I went up to them to ask if there had been any damage in the center of town.

Irwin lowered his window and smiled. "Big tree fell into the church parking lot. Good thing Mary's service was on Saturday." His voice was strong and deep, like the voice of someone who read for audio books.

"Did you see Bertha Whetmore this morning? I know you often check on her."

"Better than that. I brought her to the fire station. I'll come back later to take her home."

Irwin was an all-around nice guy, smart, good-looking. I wished he interested me.

Hank pulled the nozzle out of Irwin's tank. He was a short, stocky man with a balding head and a beard flecked with more gray than brown. His voice always sounded larger than his body but without the resonance of Irwin's. "Mary stopped at my station for gas the day she died. One of the loyal ones who don't drive five miles out of their way to save a dime. She was goin' home, goin' to have her supper. Didn't look sick. No reason she shoulda died in bed." He took cash from Irwin and disappeared into his station, a swagger of self-righteousness in his body. The generator at the side of the station was loud and smelled of gas even more than Hank did.

"I hope you won't need gas later," said Irwin. "Hank's more cranky than usual. You'd think we had a tornado instead of a blizzard. He should look around him. The world's transformed." Irwin reached over to pat the dog who was still looking out the window. "Sit, Rufus. We're going down to the lake." He started his car and put up the passenger side window. "Rufus loves to skid under the drifts on the ice. Hope you and your friend get to enjoy some snow time."

"We made snow angels last night and this morning. Right now, we're just enjoying the walk. This is Rachel Cummings. Ted's sister. She came from New Orleans for Mary's funeral."

He nodded at Rachel. "I wondered who you were at the funeral. Nice that you could come. Nicer that you got this glorious day."

"It is beautiful. Enjoy your dog walk." Rachel turned from the car and started toward the fire station.

"Here's Hank with your change," I said to Irwin. "Don't let him spoil your mood. He carries a permanent scowl on his face."

"Why we call him Hank the Crank. Don't let him spoil your mood, either. Go join your friend."

I caught up to Rachel, who was stopped on the sidewalk at the edge of the fire station parking lot. "You should go out with that guy. It's obvious that he likes you."

"I know. I wish I were interested in Irwin."

Rachel's mood had darkened. "Joseph didn't like Hank."

"I don't know anyone who likes him. But he hired Joseph every summer after his freshman year."

"He told me Hank was selling more than gas."

"Did you mention that to the police?"

"So much was happening, I don't remember what I told them. Joseph had said he'd had enough of Hank. He was going to report him to the police for selling contraband cigarettes. He might have also been selling drugs. Joseph wasn't sure."

"Did Hank know Joseph planned to report him?"

"When we left Skip's, he was going to get his bike, stop to put air in his tires, and tell Hank he quit. Maybe Hank killed Joseph."

I'd read enough mystery novels to know that murderers needed motive and opportunity. "Did he tell Hank why he was quitting?"

"Maybe."

"How would he have known that Joseph would be at the barn?"

"Maybe he saw Joseph on his bike and followed."

"That's a lot of maybes."

Jody came out of the fire station, stopping our speculations when she approached us.

"You missed breakfast." She looked at us both as if expecting some big reveal about Joseph's murder.

"We ate at my house," I said. "We're on our way to check the library. Just stopping here first to see if there's any word on when the power might be back on."

"Maybe tomorrow. Depends what part of town you live in. You're close to the center, so yours will be on before Teddy's. You staying with him, Rachel?"

"I will be." Rachel's tone was hostile toward the woman who'd told the whole town why she had come for Mary's funeral.

"She stayed with me last night. I'll be taking her back later this afternoon." I put my hand on Rachel's back and directed her away from Jody and toward the library.

When we were out of Jody's hearing, Rachel said, "Maybe we should add Jody to our list."

"She was in junior high when Joseph died. Maybe old enough to be curious, but not old enough to be out on a Friday night by herself. Let's go back to Hank. Why would he go to the barn between Friday night when we were there and Saturday after the funeral when we found the drawing in the manure hole. How could he possibly know that we had been there?"

"A logical guess. If we were looking for Joseph's murderer, we'd want to check the barn. A car went by on Friday, remember."

"So he planned to go into the barn, saw us, and came back later?"

We passed Hank's garage again. He was outside pumping gas for someone whose car I didn't recognize.

Rachel stared at Hank as we walked by. "Was he at Mary's funeral? He could have gone to the barn then."

I had seen Hank in the back pew at the funeral wearing the same hunter's jacket he always wore in winter when he pumped gas. Most days, he'd come out of the garage with one arm in a sleeve, struggling to get the other one in before he reached the pumps. He never zipped the jacket, and he hadn't zipped it at the funeral. When we all filed out of the church, I noticed that he wore a dress shirt under it. I'd never known that he liked Mary. I'd never known that he liked *anyone*. But at least he'd shown her enough respect to come. He left right after the service, plenty of time to get to the barn before Rachel and I went back and found the defaced drawing. He also lived close enough to me to have walked to my car to carve "Forget Joseph" into the snow.

We turned right to walk into the town center. "Hank and Lucille were both at the funeral," I said.

"Both still had plenty of time to get to the barn before we did."

We passed the church where the parking lot was blocked by the tree that had fallen. Three men were there using chain saws to cut it into logs that they were loading into a pick-up truck. When Seth finished at the library, he would join them and then claim some of the firewood for himself. When we got to the library, he was just finishing with the ramp.

Before we reached the walkway, Rachel said, "Was Seth at the funeral?"

"No. He resented Mary. He's always blamed her for Joseph being in the barn that day."

"That's irrational. Mary had nothing to do with it."

"Seth's not always rational. It's a good thing he never found out you'd been there with Joseph."

We stopped talking as we approached him at the top of the ramp. There were no squirrels or birds nearby for him to aim the snow at. He must have stopped at his house, because now he wore a hat with flaps that hung too far outside his ears to provide any warmth. Under the rim, beads of sweat dotted his forehead. Powerful as he was, he was eighty years old, too old to be doing so much shoveling. I vowed to find someone to take over that part of his job. Maybe Andy Carkin. I could shovel my own driveway.

We stood half-way up the ramp while Seth finished. "Snow's gettin' heavier." He threw a last shovelful over the railing.

"It's still beautiful," I said.

"Wouldn't be beautiful for the cows I used to keep. Before those health people complained." He hoisted the shovel over his shoulder in the same way Andy Carkin did.

As he squeezed his bulk past me, I asked, "Is the door open?"

"Wouldn't know. I didn't go inside." His shovel almost hit Rachel when he passed her.

I took off one of my gloves and found the library key in my pocket. When I inserted it into the lock, I didn't need to turn it.

Rachel was watching from behind me. "Seth lied? Left the door unlocked?"

"He said no."

Rachel followed me inside, closing the door behind her. "Take off your blinders, Deb. Seth could easily have found Joseph in the barn and killed him."

"Hank has a motive. Lucille may have one. Seth doesn't."

"Anger of the moment when he found another teenager in his barn. Why would he just say something about his cows? Like he's remembering the past, too."

"He wasn't keeping cows when Joseph died." I scanned the room for any sign that the storm had infiltrated the library. Everything was in order, no windows broken, no sign of a leak.

"I think he was remembering the cows because he was remembering Joseph."

I put the key into my pocket and slipped my hand back into my glove. "It's a cliché from a bad murder mystery. One of two crotchety old men killing the teenage boy."

Rachel tightened her scarf. "And one glamorous teacher. Let's get out of here. It's as cold as a tomb."

"Another cliché. But an apt one. Just let me check upstairs." I left Rachel standing in front of the checkout desk.

Upstairs was as undisturbed as downstairs. No dust bunnies had reappeared after Seth's vacuuming. The children's table was clean, the shelves arranged with just enough titles propped face out to entice young readers with their colorful covers.

When I came back downstairs, I found Rachel in my cubicle. She pointed to the desk. A chill as cold as the air in the library ran through me. Seth had been right when he left a message on my phone Friday night that my desk looked disturbed. The globe paperweight I used to hold down my to-do list was moved, the papers underneath it no longer in a neat pile. Beside them, a cloth lay bunched up as if someone had been dusting. The paperweight with its kaleidoscopic design lay on top of a book I knew too well. *Deutsch Aktuell*. I opened the cover to the yellow Post-It note I had left inside. *Gutes Raten, mein Junge*. My name glared at me in the elaborate signature I used in high school.

11

R ACHEL STOOD FROZEN in place until she spoke and her posture collapsed. "Now we'll never find his killer."

I picked up the book, wanting to bury its accusation in the library discard pile. It was too late. I couldn't change the past or send Rachel and her investigation back to New Orleans.

She stepped away from me and the book. "I'm scared."

I was more than scared. Terror, guilt, shame all coursed through my shaking body. "We need to find who's doing this."

"How?"

"We'll start with Seth and Lucille and Hank. Show each of them the book. Watch their reactions."

"Is that safe?" The past was doing more than haunting Rachel. She'd never been a coward before.

I hugged *Deutsch* to my chest and led Rachel out of the library, careful to lock the door behind me. "We'll stop at Seth's. I'll ask him about the open door. And the book."

Outside, the sun warmed our faces. I felt it against the front of my parka and through the gloves I was wearing. The center of town had come alive with people greeting each other the way people do when a blizzard has passed. Curious, even joyful after the snow's cleansing. The mood would change by nightfall when we would all tire of playing pioneers.

At the church, the men clearing the fallen tree had left only small branches littering the parking lot. Seth had missed his chance. Next to the church, his red house glowed with the sun shining on it against the snow. He'd shoveled only a narrow path to his front door. The scene could have been in a Norman Rockwell painting titled *After the Storm*.

Rachel stopped at the side of the pathway. "Go to the door. I'll wait here."

I couldn't let her give in to fear. "You're coming with me."

We walked through what felt more like a tunnel of snow than a pathway. The bell sounded loud inside when I pressed it. At the window next to the door, I saw Seth move the heavy curtain back. He motioned to us to go away. I shook my head "no" and pressed the bell again.

When he finally came to the door, his bulk covered the entire opening. "Whadaya need?"

"Can we come inside? I have some questions about the library."

"Ask them out here."

Rachel saved me from thinking up an excuse. "Deborah has questions, and I'd like to use your bathroom. I'm not used to how this cold makes me need to go. There's no bucket of water at the library to flush." When she tried flattery, I knew she'd regained the composure of her childhood. "I remember what a resourceful farmer you were. I'll bet you've got a full bucket right next to your toilet."

Seth stepped aside to let us in. "Shoulda stayed in New Hampshire 'stead of runnin' off down South. Don't know why you came back diggin' up the past. Bathroom's to the right through the bedroom. Make it fast."

Rachel walked slowly to the bathroom, pausing to glance into the kitchen. Seth kept me standing in his living room. It was dark, the curtains of both windows drawn tight against the cold outside. I gestured at a woodstove in the corner that half-warmed the room.

"I'm sorry you missed the men at the church cutting up that tree. You could have taken in a supply for your stove."

"Don't matter. I've got plenty. Whadaya want to ask me?"

"You were right. Someone was in the library on Friday. Did you see this on my desk?"

I held out the German book. He flinched and quickly stuck his hands behind his back as if he were afraid to touch it. "Never saw it. Just saw that your desk didn't look so neat as usual."

"It's a German book." I held it up so he could see the title. "Ever take German?"

His face contorted, deepening his wrinkles, and his eyes flashed hate. "Why would I do that? My uncle died fighting the Germans. My father called them dirty Krauts. Least when some of the refugees came here, they was white ones. Couldn't tell the Jews from the Christians when they came to the farm."

I'd been defending Seth as harmless. Now I wasn't so sure. If he saw Joseph with the German book, he'd have two reasons to kill him: studying German *and* hanging out in his barn. Rachel came out of the bathroom before I could say something I'd regret.

"Your friend's done. You can go now." Seth opened the door.

I moved slowly past his bulk, scanning the room for anything that could have served as a weapon. There was nothing. No pictures on the wall. No bookcase. No plants. Only a television, a worn sofa with a coffee table in front of it, a coat rack holding the jacket and hat he'd worn shoveling. Not even a memento from his days farming. I wondered what he did besides watch TV and play solitaire with the cards on the coffee table. "If you think of anything else, call me. Someone was in my office and left this book. I'd like to know who."

He backed away from the book I held out to him again, murmured "Yup," and closed the door behind us.

At the end of his tunnel-like pathway, I looked back at the house. Seth stood at the window, watching. I walked away from his gaze.

"He looked at the book like I wanted to hand him something poison."

"A *gift*." Rachel reminded me of Lucille's tribute to Joseph. "Never mind the book. There's a container in his bedroom that looks like it could have been a feeding trough for his cows. It was filled with stuff that must have come from the farm."

"Stuff?"

"Old clothes and boots. Catalogs. Lots of iron tools. Most of them looked sharp. The only thing I recognized was a set of two sickles tucked into some kind of holder."

"None of that sounds like the weapon that killed Joseph."

"The sickles had rounded wooden handles."

"Like a ball?"

"Not that big. But it was all creepy. There's a phone on his nightstand with a dish towel next to it. He could have used it to disguise his voice to call you."

"'Forget Joseph' sounded more computer generated than muffled. Did you see a computer anywhere?"

"No."

"Maybe he used one in the library." I knew that was a reach. Seth was eighty years old. He didn't even use a cell phone. I would probably cross him off of our list of suspects. Except for the German book. His reaction told me he'd seen it before.

Rachel reached over the banks of Seth's tunnel for a handful of snow. She tried to form a snowball but the sun hadn't warmed the snow enough so it would stick. She threw her handful against the pine tree in the front yard. It splattered white against the dark bark. "What now? Should we stop at Lucille's?"

"Keep walking. I'll think of an excuse to go inside."

When we reached Lucille's, her car was gone from the driveway and Andy Carkin was just starting to walk home. I called to him. "Wait up, Andy."

The road was hardpacked after the last plowing, with only a few spots of asphalt dotting the white of the snow. Andy rested his shovel against a snowbank, hanging on to it as if it were a walking stick.

"You must be exhausted."

He lifted his shovel. "Not too tired for a movie. My mom said she'd take me to one in Nashua this afternoon. Think the theater will be open?"

"I'm sure it has a generator if Nashua is still out of electricity." The theater wouldn't want to lose a profit. No matter what movie played, it would be filled with people trying to escape the cold of their houses. "Miss Larcom's car is gone. Do you know where she went? I'm guessing not to a movie."

"She just gave me five dollars and left." Andy emphasized the five dollars. Lucille had never been known for her generosity.

We stopped at the end of my driveway that Andy had worked so hard to shovel. "You're a great shoveler. Can I hire you to do the ramp at the library next storm?"

Andy beamed through his exhausted face. "Sure. I'll tell Miss Larcom I found another job. Your driveway and the library will be enough."

"Next time, I'll help you. Enjoy the movie."

Rachel watched him navigate the last stretch to his house. "Poor kid looks like he's about to fall over. Five dollars from Lucille sounds a little cheap. I wonder where she went."

"I don't know, but I know I'll give Andy ten dollars for the library. The ramp will be a lot easier than Lucille's driveway."

"What about Seth?"

"If we haven't had him arrested by then, I'll tell him it's time to let the younger generation earn money from shoveling."

My cell phone rang in my pocket as I unlocked the door. If the cell towers had been affected by the storm, they were working now.

Modern technology never quit. A beep told me someone left a message.

We took our boots off at the kitchen door and went into the living room where the fire was dying down. I rested my cell phone on the barrel that served as my coffee table.

Rachel hung up her parka and took mine. "You'll have to check that message."

"In a minute." I picked up our dirty oatmeal bowls and carried them into the kitchen. The snow in the pan had only half melted. Like my relationship with Rachel. I went back into the living room where she was standing in front of the half-lit woodstove.

"We need to warm this place up," I said. She moved behind the barrel while I put two logs into the stove. They caught, creating a landscape of red, yellow, and orange flames.

Rachel looked at my phone as if it, too, were on fire. "Listen to the message."

When I pressed the home button, Nathan and Cathy, heads touching, smiled at me. I'd had the same screen saver ever since I learned how to crop and save an old photo of my husband and child and scan it into my phone and computer. The image was fuzzy but it kept them sharp in my memory. I blew a silent kiss at them, swiped the phone on, and pressed the receiver icon. The screen told me I had one voice message. No name was attached to the number.

I released the muscles that were knotting around my stomach when I heard, "Deborah, this is Holly Hoche. I'm Mary Wheeler's executor. Please call me to set up a meeting about her will."

I set the phone on the barrel and motioned Rachel to sit down. "It was Mary's executor." Beethoven had claimed my chair. I picked him up and held him in my lap while I took his place. I could feel his warmth through my jeans. He purred against my hands.

Rachel leaned forward in her chair to get closer to the warmth of the fire. "Why did Mary's executor call you?"

"It's Holly Hoche. She wants to set up a meeting."

"But why with you?"

"Maybe because she knows I check on Mary's house. I'm calling her back now."

I pressed the call back button. Holly answered quickly. "Thanks for calling. I'm sitting here in my office with a heater plugged into a generator that's keeping me warm, and I'm catching up on work even though it's Sunday. Do you have power?"

"No, but we're staying warm by my woodstove."

"We?" The generator hummed behind Holly's voice like a mechanical echo of Beethoven's purring. It reminded me of the mechanical message to "Forget Joseph," though Holly had been a toddler when he died.

"Rachel Cummings. She came for the funeral."

"That's helpful."

"Helpful how?" Beethoven jumped off my lap. I moved my free hand behind my back to keep in some of his warmth.

"You're both in Mary's will. And Ted. Can you all meet me tomorrow? Ten o'clock at Mary's house?"

I nodded at Rachel. "Rachel and I can. We'll ask Teddy."

"Ten o'clock then. Let's hope the power's back on. Otherwise, her house will feel like a tomb." She hung up before I could comment on her metaphor.

Rachel started to twist her hair, something she hadn't done since we made our snow angels. "You and me and Teddy. What's that all about?"

"Apparently we're in Mary's will. Call Teddy. Ask if he can meet with Holly at ten tomorrow."

"My phone's upstairs." She rose out of her chair and left the room, her usual grace lost under footsteps that now sounded heavy on the floor even in her stocking feet.

I waited, listening to the sounds of the empty room. The fire sparked, but it didn't throw out enough heat to warm me. I heard Beethoven scratch in his litter box. Outside, someone's brakes squealed. I went to the window, but the driver gunned the engine and sped away before I got there. A visible skid showed on the road where the snow was turning to slush. I looked at Mary's house. Against the snow that was pristine in her yard, its white paint looked dingy. Anyone who thought white was one shade hadn't lived through a snowstorm.

I heard Rachel descend the stairs. She came into the room holding her phone to her ear. She shook her head. "Teddy's not answering."

"Maybe he's outside checking on the cabins he has for his workers. Or just walking around. That's my best therapy when I get too sad."

"Does that happen often?"

I stood in front of the woodstove warming my back. "After Nathan and Cathy died, I moved through depression to melancholy. Now I've found that I'm even capable of joy. As long as I get enough time outside."

"You always were an outdoor person. Where do you go?"

"For walks around the lake or up Musket Hill. I have a couple of friends I hike with. Sometimes we climb Mount Monadnock or go into Massachusetts and walk around Walden Pond. Once a year, we hike in the White Mountains and stay in one of the huts."

"Friends. Do I know them?"

"No. Lisa and Ann. They bought the old Gardner house about fifteen years ago. Lisa teaches at Nashua High School and Ann teaches at Graniteville Elementary."

"Lesbians?"

I moved away from the stove. "I assume so. I never felt the need to ask."

"At least we've made some progress. I'll try Teddy again after lunch. Should we find a restaurant that's open?"

"We could go to the fire station," I said, though I cringed at the idea of eating with nosey townspeople.

"Too many people who'll stare at me."

I did a mental inventory of my cabinets. "I've got bread, peanut butter, jelly."

"I haven't eaten pb & j since that day we road our bikes to the barn."

"Eat it now. It will help to exorcise your ghost." I went into the kitchen to make our sandwiches, leaving Rachel to sit near the fire pretending it was warm.

When I came back with the sandwiches on paper plates, she was sitting with our yearbook in her lap. I wished I had put it back in my closet instead of leaving it on the bookshelf. I took it from her and gave her a sandwich. "We can look at this later. First we should eat and call Teddy again."

We ate in silence. I often fixed myself peanut butter and jelly without remembering what Rachel reminded me of. We'd packed it for our lunches the day Joseph died. I forced myself to swallow what felt like paste in my mouth. I got up to pour us the little fresh water that was left in the jug in the downstairs bathroom. When I handed a glass to Rachel, she drank it down fast. She'd eaten only half her sandwich.

She set glass and paper plate on the barrel. "I can't eat any more."

I hadn't made it through much more of my own sandwich. "Neither can I. Call Teddy. He'll feed us something if we get hungry."

Rachel pressed Teddy's number. She waited a long time before hanging up. "I'll try Janet and Elizabeth." She waited again for his wife, then for his daughter to answer. "No one's near a cell phone. Maybe they went out to find some place to eat."

"Teddy hates restaurants."

"That's because after my mother died, we went out to eat a lot. Our father always got drunk."

There was nothing I could say to that. I could help her search for Joseph's murderer, but I couldn't undo the damage of her childhood. "It's cold in here and we have nothing else to do. Go get your things and I'll take you back to Teddy's. At least it'll be warm in the car."

Rachel went upstairs for her overnight bag. When she came down, her face was pale.

"What's wrong?"

"I remember why I can't eat peanut butter."

"Why?"

"Joseph was allergic to peanuts."

"Peanuts didn't kill him." I took our parkas down from the hooks above the woodstove. We put on hats, scarves, boots. When I locked the kitchen door, I heard my Princess phone ring. It could ring all afternoon and no one would be able to leave a message to invade an empty room.

12

I WAS THANKFUL for my snow tires when I turned at Teddy's farm stand onto the dirt road that led to his house. Hank might be cranky and he might have let hundreds of his tires float down the river, but he didn't overcharge me when he changed my tires for the winter and summer seasons. The town plow had made only one swipe on the road. I followed what looked like tire tracks from Teddy's truck. If he'd gone out, he had already come back, because the tracks went both ways.

We passed the barn where the cow now wore a cap of snow. Her watching eyes looked wet from the cap's melting.

Rachel asked me to stop. "She looks like she's crying."

"I used to say that to my parents if we went past it in the rain. Cow still seems more alive than wooden to me."

"If she could talk, she'd tell us who killed Joseph. We should go inside again. See if anyone's been there since yesterday."

Rachel fidgeted with the scarf Elizabeth had knitted. Her agitation had increased ever since we started back to Teddy's. I tried to calm her by driving past the barn slowly so I could study the snow around it. "No one's been there. There are no tire tracks or footprints." The tree branches along the road were pulled down by the snow. "Praying trees," I said.

"You still call them that?"

"Ever since Teddy made up that phrase."

Rachel stopped fingering the scarf and looked out the window so I could barely hear what she said. "It was actually Eric Donaldson who said that. Then he shook the snow off all the trees around us. The balls of snow on the ground looked like bullets. What did Lucille ever find attractive in him?"

"Youth, vitality, sex. If she was sleeping with Eric in high school, Joseph probably knew it. Reason enough to kill him if she thought he might start telling others about it. Teenage boys talk a lot about sex."

"Joseph didn't gossip."

I wanted to solve his murder, but I also wanted to tell her to stop thinking of him as *Saint* Joseph. I kept my eyes on the road. The cabins built for the Jamaicans appeared in a thinner grove of trees. The snow reached half-way up the clapboards that Teddy had painted a forest green. If I hadn't known they were there, I might have missed them. Wherever Teddy went earlier, he hadn't check the cabins.

We rounded a curve to the open fields that would be covered in corn in another six months. Our answer to the whereabouts of Teddy and his family glided on cross-country skis toward us. I wished I were skiing with them. Rachel opened her window and waved, letting the cold air waft into the car.

When I parked behind Teddy's truck, I saw that its wheels were splattered with snow. I found the lever to my trunk and popped it open to get Rachel's suitcase. "We shouldn't have worried about no one answering the phone."

"Wait on that suitcase. If Teddy can't meet with Holly Hoche tomorrow, I'll stay with you again. We can talk with Lucille and Hank the Crank." She got out of the car and slammed the trunk closed.

I could see her shaking when we climbed the steps to the front porch and the plaque that read 1856. Someone had swept the snow off the green paint of the floorboards. The porch was empty of the Adirondack chairs I remembered seeing in the barn. The front of the house was perfectly balanced, a heavy wooden door painted the same forest green as the Jamaican cabins, the windows on either side of the door painted with matching trim. Between each window and the door, Teddy had hung old farm implements, a pitch fork on one side, a spade on the other.

Rachel touched the pitch fork. "It looks like a weapon."

She needed to stop thinking about murder, to enjoy a visit with her brother. "If anyone drove this far out of town to break in, they'd find nothing to steal. Teddy's a farmer, more Robert Frost than wealthy developer. The only thing in the house worth stealing are Janet's quilts."

Rachel opened the door easily. No one in the family ever locked it. Inside was dark and cold, the porch blocking out sunlight that streamed from the front windows when the sun was lower in the morning. A good layout for the summer, but dreary for the short January days. Nothing in the living room had changed since I bought tomato starts from Teddy. Three of Janet's quilts decorated the walls. The blankets she knitted were rumpled on the chairs and sofa instead of being neatly draped over them. Teddy, Janet, and Elizabeth must have wrapped themselves in them to add warmth to the weak heat coming from the fire that now smoldered in the woodstove. We took off our boots and moved toward the stove. Rachel stoked it and added two more logs. We were standing in front of it warming our backs when we heard the skiers come in through the kitchen door.

Elizabeth came into the living room first, her face a healthy reddish brown from being outside. "You need to go play in the snow, Aunt Rachel. It's perfect for skiing." She shed a factory-made hat and scarf.

Rachel took off the ones Elizabeth had knitted. "Should we trade?"

"No. You need to keep those as long as you're here."

Rachel tugged off the cheap gloves she'd bought at Walmart, stuffed them in her pockets, and wrapped the scarf around her neck again. Elizabeth seemed to calm her. "You're an excellent knitter. I was plenty warm when Deb and I made snow angels."

"I love making snow angels! You should go skiing, then you can both hang out with us. Borrow my mom's skis. Deb can use mine. The ski boots should fit close enough." Elizabeth offered what I was craving. She hung her parka on a hook over the stove and set her hat, scarf, and gloves on the hearth. Her technique was a mirror of my own. She picked up the blanket from the chair she claimed as hers and sank into it.

Janet and Teddy came into the room. They copied Elizabeth's arrangement of her ski clothes. "Have lunch with us, then borrow our skis." Janet had been listening from the kitchen. "I can use my gas stove to heat the extra stew I didn't take to Mary's funeral."

Rachel looked out the window at the snow field across the road.

Janet was standing in front of a bookcase that held the photo of Teddy and Joseph that Rachel had used for her drawing of Joseph's face. Next to it, a bookend kept the books upright. I'd seen that design before. Mahogany. The angled pedestal holding a rounded ball with a handle. They must have been popular years ago because I remembered one in my grandparents' house. My grandmother called the set her cannonball bookends.

I tried to focus on Janet instead of the photo and the bookend that looked like a weapon. Snow sparkled in her hair as if it were studded with diamonds. Her dark skin glowed from the fresh air and the cold. "Did you go into town to check things out?"

"Teddy did. Before Elizabeth and I managed to crawl out of bed in the cold."

Teddy came into the room and stood next to his wife, his face pale against her dark one, his posture so stiff he could have been frozen in place. "It was warm in my truck. I just drove around a bit. Saw a few trees down. One blocking the church parking lot. Everything was quiet, the way it gets after a storm. I didn't turn on my radio and I didn't see another car. The world should always feel that way."

Janet defended his driving around. "He checked on Bertha Whetmore."

Bertha was confused enough lately that I worried about her. "Does she need some place to stay?" I asked. "She shouldn't be alone in a house without electricity."

Teddy moved away from Janet and stood in front of the bookcase. "She refuses to leave, says she's lived through a hundred snowstorms that knocked out electricity. I stoked her fire, made sure she still knew how to add wood to it safely, and that she had a couple of jugs of water in her bathroom."

"Did she?" She was so frail I doubted she could lift even a small log.

"She was well-prepared. She's stronger than you think. And stubborn as hell."

"Hard to convince someone like her to accept help." I thought of my parents who needed to start accepting what I offered.

"She'll be fine. Before I left, Irwin Trombly stopped to check on her. He promised to keep looking in."

This was why I loved Shelby. Neighbors helping neighbors... or *killing* them, I thought as I looked at the picture of Joseph behind Teddy. I touched the bookend next to it. It felt loose. "These bring back memories. My grandparents had a set like this."

"I need to glue that one." He slid the photo further away from it. "I'm guessing you're more interested in this photo. You and Rachel need to forget Joseph. The case is closed. We've all moved on. Go skiing. It's peaceful out in the field."

I wished I had gotten up earlier, gone for a walk, watched the animals instead of the people. "The peace is already breaking up. The fire station is bustling with people getting food and water."

Janet tossed back her head. The drops from the melting snow glittered in her hair. "Go try on the boots. Ski off those old wounds Mary's death has opened up."

"Opened for all of us," said Rachel, who walked with her brother into the kitchen.

Janet and I stayed another minute looking at the photo. "He's never gotten over Joseph's death. He'll calm down in a bit. Rachel's brought back too many memories."

"It was a terrible time. You're lucky you didn't live through it." I left her with Elizabeth, who had been listening curiously.

I went into the kitchen where Teddy was pulling the door closed with one hand, a pot of stew he'd taken out of a snowbank in the other. He set it on top of the gas stove. "Try the boots on. Get to your skiing while it's still nice out."

Rachel and I each picked up a pair and sat on kitchen chairs to try them on. The laces were as cold as my hands. I'd warm up when I started to move in the sun. "Before we go out, we need to ask you something."

"Who needs to ask? You or Rachel?"

"Both of us," said Rachel. "My boots fit. Yours, Deb?"

"Perfect." I faced Teddy as I zipped my parka. "Holly Hoche wants to meet us tomorrow morning at Mary's. Something about her will."

Teddy lit the burner. "What's her will got to do with us?"

"She didn't say. Just that she wants to meet us." I fixed my hat so it covered my ears.

"No can do. You'll have to go without me."

Rachel marched her feet to check the fit of her boots. "Do you mind if I stay another night with Deb? Then we can just walk across the street for the meeting."

"That's fine. Go skiing now. We'll save you some stew if you're hungry when you finish." He left the kitchen and I heard him talking with Elizabeth in the living room.

Outside, Rachel and I and found the skis resting on the side of the house. "Do you think he's really busy tomorrow?" I asked. "He seems stressed."

"We're feeding off each other. Don't forget that Joseph was his best friend. Wounds like ours scab over but they never really heal."

Rachel was more right than she knew. The last time I cross-country skied with Nathan, I had just learned that I was pregnant with Cathy. I never told Rachel that Cathy was born on the same date that Joseph died.

We reached the edge of the field and stepped into our skis. I started to follow the single set of tracks. They were perfectly parallel, like two pretzel sticks laid side by side. Ahead, they became confused where the leader switched, then they straightened out again. The entire right side of the field was marked this way. Parallel lines punctuated with switching points where the order was disturbed like the way our lives had been interrupted by Rachel's return.

I glided away from the tracks to make my own. Rachel fell farther behind me. I lifted my left ski, then my right to pivot around to her. "Are you okay?"

"Concentrating. I used to love skiing, now I barely remember how to maneuver one ski in front of the other."

"Do you want to go back?"

"And miss this?" She pointed to a flock of small birds that circled a stray corn stalk peeking through the snow. Chickadees or nuthatches. They were too far away to identify. The sun shadowed their silhouettes onto the white. The snow-covered field unfolded toward them, undisturbed by the ski tracks that veered to the right.

"Let's go as far as that stalk, tag it, and make a wish."

My legs were tired despite the tracks broken into the snow. A good kind of tired. The cleansing power of exercising in nature.

"Do you want to break trail?" Rachel needed to channel her energy.

"I'll lead back."

I pushed forward, my skis plowing more than gliding. The sun was warm enough that I loosened my scarf and unzipped my parka. By the time we reached the corn stalk, the birds had flown away. Seed kernels dotted the snow around it. I touched the stalk and wished for healing. I couldn't change that I left Joseph's German book in the barn. Rachel couldn't change that she went there with him the night he was murdered. Whether we found his killer or not, we could accept our guilt and recreate our friendship.

Rachel picked up some snow and showered it over our heads. "A purifying." She seemed less frantic as she placed her skis in the parallel tracks I'd made and glided rather than plowed away. Her back was tall and straight. She could have been an Egyptian gliding across the desert.

In the distance, I heard the noise of an engine. Teddy was backing his truck out of the driveway, maybe going to find quiet from the women invading his house.

13

WE PROPPED OUR skis at the side of Teddy's house and went inside. Janet and Elizabeth were in the living room, huddled near the woodstove, wrapped in blankets, and reading books.

"Don't get up. You'll get cold again," I said. "We're heading back to my house to do the same thing. Did Teddy go into town?"

"To the fire station for water, even though we have enough for two more days." Janet rested her book on the blanket and her hands under it. *The Good Braider*. I knew Terry Farish's story in verse about a Sudanese girl in Maine learning to become an American. Janet had brought Elizabeth to the library the evening Terry came down from Maine to give a reading. I wondered if Janet felt herself the kind of outsider to Shelby the way the girl felt in Portland, or if she bought it for Elizabeth to identify with her black heritage.

Rachel tousled Elizabeth's hair. "Pleasure or school?" She touched the copy of *Jane Eyre* Elizabeth held in her lap.

"Both. I just got to the part where Jane rescues Rochester from his bed that's on fire."

Bertha set the fire. The madwoman in the attic, the character Rochester had hidden away. The one who always made me think of Bertha Whetmore. The one I felt like when Nathan and Cathy died. The woman who had no happy ending. "I won't spoil it for you by giving you a hint about how the fire started. I'll bring your Aunt

Rachel back tomorrow afternoon. It wouldn't surprise me if you finished the book by then. It's a great day for reading."

We left Janet and Elizabeth where we found them. When we got into my car, we felt how much it had been warmed by the sun shining in its front window. It was warmer than Teddy's kitchen, warm enough that Rachel removed her hat and clutched it in her lap. She let go of it briefly to point to three deer trying to run through the snow in the field. "They should have skis on. Teddy's lucky. He's surrounded by nature and a beautiful family. I wonder if I'd have stayed here if I married Joseph." Her anxiety was turning into romanticizing the past.

"Most people don't marry their high school sweethearts." I had long ago left romance for realism.

She stopped playing with the hat when she noticed a piece of yarn starting to unravel. "Most people's high school sweethearts don't get murdered."

"Quit playing with the hat. I can fix it when we get to my house."

"Are we going straight back?"

"We'll stop at the fire station for fresh water, then at Hank's. I need gas. You can use the bathroom excuse again and look around."

We drove in silence along the road that had become slushy. By morning it would be frozen mud. Teddy was just leaving the fire station when we pulled in for water. He waved and drove on. "He's been a good brother to you," I said to Rachel.

"I couldn't have survived without him. Not just because of Joseph. I don't know why he was going to party the night Joseph died. He doesn't drink now and he didn't drink then. He'd seen too much of what it did to our father." She watched the truck skid as it pulled out of the parking lot. The space it left empty opened a view of the firehouse door. "Get out of the car. She's over there."

Lucille. She was carrying a plastic jug of water in each hand. I handed Rachel a glass jar that had once held pickles for the church fair. I carried a second jar to Lucille at her car. "Everything okay at your house?"

Lucille opened the back door to the mini-Cooper convertible she drove. "Same as everybody's. No water, no heat, no lights. School's already canceled for tomorrow, so I'm going into Nashua to stay with Brendan. He's got a generator. He'll keep me warm."

Brendan was a new biology teacher at the high school. He was thirty to Lucille's fifty. The way she spoke made me think she'd found another relationship with a younger man. She wore no hat over her styled hair. Her lipstick and eyeliner were the same shade of reddish-brown.

"Rachel and I are going to open a can of chicken soup, warm it on my gas stove, and read our books until it gets dark." I threw out the first German title I could think of. "I'm half-way into *Death in Venice*."

"I struggled through that one."

"Did you read it in German? I wish I didn't have to use a translation."

"I did. Then I quit German."

"Do you remember the German book we used in high school? *Deutsch Aktuell.*"

Lucille raised one of the water jugs as if she wanted to hit me with it. "How can you remember that far back?"

"I found a copy on my desk in the library today."

"Maybe they still use it. I don't pay attention to the German class." Lucille got into her car, bending low so her head wouldn't hit the top of the mini-Cooper, whose rust color matched her hair almost as well as her lipstick. The car was stylish, but I never understood why anyone taller than five feet would want to own one.

"Maybe someone knew what Deb was reading. Left her a gift to help with her German." Rachel emphasized the word "gift."

We both jumped when the fire siren sounded. Seconds later, two trucks emerged from the station, their lights flashing, their sirens blaring. Lucille got into her car and pulled away from the truck just in time. When the road was clear, she drove away, saved from any need to respond to Rachel's taunt.

Hank came out of his gas station, one arm in the sleeve of his jacket, the other finding its second sleeve.

"Stay here. Forget the bathroom excuse," I said to Rachel. I got out of the car and met Hank before he reached the pumps.

"You need gas? Getting out of town with that friend of yours? Don't know why she came all the way here just for a funeral." His face was fixed in his Hank-the-Crank scowl.

"Mary was good to her when she and Teddy were kids. They were friends with Joseph."

"Joseph?"

"Mary's son. You hired him to work summers."

"Forgot his name." Hank was lying. Even if he'd forgotten Joseph's name before, he would have remembered it after yesterday's funeral. "How much gas do you want?"

"Fill me up. Can I go inside? I need cigarettes."

"When'd you take up smoking?"

I lifted my chin toward the car. "Rachel smokes. But not in my car. I hate the smell."

"Why don't she get her own cigarettes?"

"We were cross-country skiing. She twisted her ankle."

"Stupid sport. Go ahead inside. You can pay for the cigarettes with the gas. Cash only. I got the best prices around." Hank walked toward my car. Rachel kept her head bent down as if she were reading a book.

I went inside to the smell of oil coming from the repair shop and permeating the tiny space Hank called his office. The door was open to the shop that I'd been inside a few times when he changed my tires. It held a bay and a lift for only one car. A back wall was lined with cartons of cigarettes, enough that, if Joseph had been right, Hank was still getting illegally. If he was also selling drugs, none were visible. The side walls held a variety of tire gauges, windshield wiper blades, oil cans, small tools. A hammer with a ball-like end sat next to a box filled with window washer. I picked it up and jumped back when I heard Hank behind me.

His deep voice boomed at me. "What do you want with that ball peen hammer?"

"I never saw a hammer like this."

"I use it for knocking out dents. Put it back and come into the office. That's where the cigarettes are."

"I need window washer, too."

"Go get your cigarettes and I'll fill your reservoir." He grabbed an open jug of fluid and waited for me to go into his office. I watched his squat body and balding head go to my car. Cartons of a variety of cigarettes sat on the shelf along with the cash register and a computer. I picked up a carton of Marlboros, hoping he'd let me buy just one pack.

I felt air as cold as his voice when he came back inside. "You hardly needed any fluid. I sell those by the carton."

"How much?"

"Sixty-five dollars."

I was shocked at the price. "I'll get a single pack somewhere else. I want Rachel to break the habit."

"You won't find them cheaper anywhere. I keep my cigarettes at least ten dollars lower than the competition and make up for it with my gas prices."

Hank's gas was always a few cents more than the other service stations. I paid the extra for the convenience, and paid a little more by having to listen to his crankiness. His voice followed me out the door after I paid him for the gas and window washer. "Tell Rachel to forget Joseph. Let the dead rest in peace."

I flicked the light switch in my kitchen before I remembered that I had no electricity. The room was dim from the lowering sun. And *cold*. We kept our coats on and went into the living room where Beethoven was curled asleep on my chair. My Princess phone sat unblinking next to my cordless phone. Whoever had called when we left the house couldn't leave a message.

I stoked the fire and loaded it with wood. "Should we drive into Nashua? See if there's any place open for dinner?"

Rachel grabbed a blanket from the back of the empty chair and plopped herself down. "I'd rather stay here. You said you had cans of soup."

"Chicken noodle. I keep a few cans in my cabinet. If I get the flu when my parents are in Florida, there's no one to nurse me and bring me chicken soup."

"That'll do. I'm too tired to move."

"Not used to playing in the snow?"

I could see her shaking under the blanket that might protect her from the cold but wasn't protecting her from the past. "Not used to tracking down a murderer. Seth or Hank? Or Lucille, even though Bertha wrote 'he,' not 'she'?"

I left the door to the woodstove open, lifted Beethoven off the chair he'd warmed, and held him on my lap. "Joseph was right about Hank selling cheap cigarettes, though sixty-five dollars a carton doesn't sound cheap to me. He had something called a ball peen hammer."

"What's that?"

"A hammer with one rounded end. He said he uses it to knock out dents."

126

"Did it have blood on it?"

"I didn't look that closely. Any trace of Joseph would be long gone by now anyway. It was thirty years ago."

"Doesn't feel like it." She bent her legs onto the chair and hugged her knees to her chest.

"I know. Seth and Lucille both have motives. Hank has a weapon."

"And opportunity, if Joseph stopped at his station before he went to the barn and told him why he was quitting."

Beethoven jumped off my lap. I quickly missed his warmth. All I wanted to do was crawl into bed, pull the covers over my head, and wake up to a new day when I wasn't searching for the answer to a case as cold as the air that was penetrating the walls. "Let's stop thinking about it. It's cold. It's getting dark. There's nothing else we can do today. How about soup and a game of Scrabble? Then we can use our headlamps to read in bed."

Rachel lowered her legs to the floor. Her feet stuck out from the blanket. A piece of hay was caught on one of the woolen socks she wore, a reminder of her shrine to Joseph. "I suppose you'll clobber me worse than when we were in high school."

I stood up to find the Scrabble game I kept on a lower shelf of my bookcase. "I'm pretty rusty. I haven't found a good partner. If I want a game, I play solitaire." I thought of the deck of cards on Seth's coffee table. I shivered not from the cold but from the fear that I'd become like him or Bertha, someone old and lonely with no one to care enough to ask if I wanted company. Or chicken soup.

I tossed in bed listening for sounds in the night. The owl in the tree outside my window whoo'd into the silence. Beethoven jumped on my bed and curled against my feet. Rachel cried out in her sleep. Toward morning, I heard the furnace kick on. We'd get up to a warm house and a new day.

14

THE ELECTRICITY HAD come on in Mary's house along with the heat, but it was still cold. I boosted up the thermostat, wishing we hadn't decided that we could walk across the street without putting on jackets. I switched on a floor lamp. It was old, brass with a fringed lampshade, the bulb wattage just enough to shed extra light onto the spot Mary used to lie on to read. When I sat on it, it still seemed to hold the imprint of her athletic body. A strand of dark brown hair curled around one of the three-petaled fabric flowers that dotted the beige background of the arm rest. Mary often dozed on the sofa after her school day. I lifted the hair and twirled it between my thumb and finger before I put it into my pocket, willing it to guide me through the grief her death had rekindled.

Rachel paced around the room. "It hasn't changed since we used to hang out here."

She was right. Prints of a half-a-dozen composers framed in cherry wood hung against the off-white walls. Mary's baby grand piano took up half the room, its top open, the music she had been playing before she died just visible to me above the keyboard. The bookshelf behind the piano held more music than books. A few photos were arranged on the mantle over her fireplace. One was her wedding picture, a twenty-one year old Mary smiling from under a bridal veil that had been pulled back to reveal her face. Beside her, the groom looked like the son he would never meet. The other pictures were of Joseph, alone, or with Rachel or Teddy or me. None showed that Mary ever had a relationship with Conrad Donaldson.

A car stopped outside. Rachel looked out the window, her black hair and the black sweater she was wearing framed by the muslin ball-fringed curtains Mary hung at almost every window. We used to laugh that she was fixated on the old-fashioned. "Goes with the house," she'd tell us.

Rachel moved away from the window to the front door. "She's here. Medium height. Hair shorter than yours. One of those pixie cuts. She's wearing a black coat and fashion boots. Carrying a briefcase. More black-clad lawyer than rose-colored Hollyhock."

"Don't talk like Seth Thompson. Holly hates being called that."

Rachel opened the door and held out her hand. "You must be Holly Hoche. I'm Rachel." When she closed the door, she turned to me and winked at how nicely she'd pronounced Holly's last name.

Rachel was right. Holly looked like a lawyer instead of the jean-clad young woman who often came to the library asking for the latest John Grisham or Scott Turow novel. "Can I take your coat? I cranked up the heat. I'll be sure to lower it when we leave."

Holly set the briefcase onto the coffee table in front of the sofa. She put a large canvas bag on top of it and took off the coat that she let fall onto the sofa. Her wool dress edged its gray across tights the same black as her boots. Professional, with a hairstyle that demanded nothing but a comb. She was like Rachel. Even when she wore jeans, she managed to look glamorous.

"Let's meet in the kitchen. I brought pastries for us." Holly's voice was crisp, a reminder to anyone listening that she was in charge.

We followed her into the kitchen where sunlight streamed through a back window that Mary had never covered with curtains.

Rachel found a chair at the table where the sun would warm

her back. "I must have sat at this table a thousand times. Nothing's changed." Her voice cracked.

I took a chair next to hers. She was right that nothing had changed. The stove and refrigerator might be different but they were still white against the pine cabinets and counter top that had been built in the nineteenth century. The wood was nicked with a hundred and fifty years of cooking and living. The carpet sample in front of the sink changed every few years, but it always had some kind of intricate flower pattern that wouldn't show spills. The rest of the oak floor was bare, the table and four chairs a pine stained in the same amber shade as the cabinets. It felt like Mary should still be alive waiting to serve us pastries that she'd baked herself.

Holly filled a tea kettle with water from a bottle she took out of the canvas bag, and rummaged through the cabinets for plates and the bone china cups Mary collected. She lifted a wooden tea carrier from the counter and held it out to us. "I knew the water was shut off. But there's tea. Three choices. There's no milk but there's a pot of sugar on the counter."

I knew what was in each lidded pot. Sugar in the small one, wheat flour in the medium, white flour in the large one. Everything was familiar except for a kitchen without Mary. We chose our tea while Holly found plates and arranged the pastries.

The tea kettle whistled into the empty air. We settled ourselves with our cups and an apple pastry while Holly opened her briefcase. She took out an official looking document. "Mary's will. She updated it just three months ago."

"Why?" I sipped peppermint tea, wishing it were a mug of strong coffee.

"She didn't say. Just asked me to take Lucille Larcom out and leave you three in."

Rachel held one hand around her tea cup. It almost circled the whole circumference. "We *three*?"

"You, Deborah, and Ted."

I bit into the pastry. It was a little too sweet, but moist and spiced with cinnamon. Mary had no heirs. Were we suddenly going to own her house and all her retirement funds? That didn't seem likely. She once told me that her estate would go to a scholarship fund for a promising music student.

Holly confirmed my memory. "Mary's house will be sold. The proceeds and what money she had will establish a scholarship fund for a graduating senior planning to study music in college. It will be a sizeable amount. The house is paid off and she's been buying IRAs to supplement what the fund will get from her years teaching."

Rachel began twisting a strand of hair, leaving a few crumbs from her pastry in it. "Was Lucille Larcom supposed to inherit her estate?"

Holly finished chewing a bit of pastry. "I shouldn't have mentioned Lucille. I can't say more."

I tried another approach. "I noticed a few months ago that Mary was avoiding Lucille. Do you know what happened?"

Rachel stopped twisting her hair and picked up her tea cup. "Are we inheriting what Lucille was supposed to have?"

"All I can say is that Deborah gets Mary's car and her piano."

"Why the piano? I don't play." I wasn't sure I wanted to trade my Prius for Mary's Subaru and pay Hank's gas prices. I didn't know where I could store her piano. I'd have to hire someone to get it upstairs until I found someone who wanted it.

"She stipulated that Deborah find a former student who planned to pursue a music career. Or wait until one does."

"That's not all," said Rachel. "Where do Teddy and I come in?"

"The three of you are to walk through the house before it goes up for sale. That's why I wanted to meet you here instead of in my Nashua office. Take anything you want. The rest will get auctioned off."

I looked down at the floral pattern of my tea cup. Too delicate for my taste. I ran my hand over the table whose craftsmanship I'd always envied. "Why us?"

"I asked Mary that. She said that after her son died, you were like children to her."

Rachel pushed aside her half-eaten pastry. "But I haven't seen her in thirty years."

"She told me you once confided in her. She couldn't help you then, but it helped her to know that you trusted her in a difficult time."

Rachel stood up and brought her dishes to the sink. I'd get them later and wash them at my house.

"Is that all?" said Rachel, her voice a secretive mumble.

"She didn't betray your confidence, if that's what you mean. Sit back down. There's more." Holly shook her head at me. She seemed unsure about how to respond to Rachel.

Rachel returned to the table and steadied herself by holding the back of her chair. "Just tell us what else and then we can go home."

Holly scanned the second page of Mary's will. "She asks one thing of you all."

I feared the request would be to find Joseph's murderer. "All of us? Me, Rachel, and Teddy?"

"She wants the three of you to take her ashes and bury them at Joseph's grave."

I reached for Rachel who had sat down again next to me. Her hand was as cold as ice. "We can't do that until the snow melts."

Holly put Mary's will back in its envelope. "You can choose when to bury the ashes. I called Pastor Pam this morning. She left them at the church along with all the photographs from the funeral. If she's not there when you need them, you can ask Seth Thompson to let you in."

Rachel pushed my hand away. "I don't want to do this."

132

Holly stood to leave. "You should respect Mary's wishes, but I can't force you. I've done my job. Take anything you want from the house. Or leave a tag. Someone will be coming next week to empty it out."

We went into the living room and watched Holly put on her coat, then go outside to get into her car. Rachel collapsed on the sofa, releasing tears she'd been holding back ever since we entered Mary's house. While she sobbed beside me, I closed my eyes and tried to figure out why Mary would have disinherited Lucille. Had she somehow discovered that Lucille killed Joseph? Why, then, wouldn't she have told the police?

It was an hour before Rachel calmed herself enough to move off the sofa. We found our way to Joseph's room. Rachel lay face down on his bed. It was the same single bed without a headboard, but the spread was different. The entire room was different. Mary hadn't kept it as a shrine. A sewing machine and flat table held pieces of the table runners she was working on when she died. She supplied the town Christmas fair with runners, napkins, tea cozies, and aprons. They always sold out and she'd already started on next year's supply. I gathered the few pieces she'd finished to store for next Christmas. I opened the drawers to the one dresser and found only scrap material and spare linen. The closet was empty. I sat on the bed next to Rachel and massaged her neck. "There's nothing here. Get up now and I'll take you to Teddy's. We'll look through the house with him when we take the ashes to the cemetery."

We went downstairs and out the door, planning to hurry across the street because we had no jackets. Lucille was standing in front of my mailbox. When she saw us, she thrust something into the box.

Rachel charged across the street in front of a car that barely missed her. She ignored the driver's horn and grabbed Lucille. Lucille was shorter than Rachel but strong. If they fought, Lucille would probably win the battle.

When I reached them, Rachel was yelling. "What did you put in her mailbox?"

Lucille yelled back, her voice more shrill than usual. "It's none of your business, Rachel. Go back to wherever it is you live. Mary's dead and buried."

"Not buried. We're burying her ashes with Joseph."

Lucille thrust her chin toward Mary's house. "What were you doing in there?"

I opened my mailbox and took out the paper without reading it. "Talking with Holly Hoche about Mary's will. Do you know anything about it?"

Lucille's anger had turned her face as red as her hair. Now it drained of color. "Why would I know that? I wasn't her confidante. You weren't either. Why'd that lawyer want you?"

"She cut you—"

I stopped Rachel before she finished. "Mary put a clause in her will asking that Rachel and Teddy and I bury her ashes with Joseph."

The color came slowly back into Lucille's face. "She got obsessed with her will a few months ago, but that's crazy. She didn't know she was going to die. She wouldn't know that Rachel would come for her funeral. Wouldn't know she'd die in January when the ground is frozen solid."

"She'd know that Teddy would contact Rachel whenever she did die. We were the closest she had to family after Joseph died. She left instructions for us to take anything we want from her house. Everything else goes to a scholarship fund. Did you know that?"

"How would I know that? She didn't talk to me about her will."

Rachel confronted her. "You're lying. You just said she had become obsessed with her will."

Lucille waited a moment before she said, "Obsessed with *having* one. She didn't say what she wanted to put in it. Go inside. You'll catch your own deaths standing out here in the cold without coats. Mail carrier hasn't come yet," she said as she started back toward her house.

I looked down at the note and read, "The past is over. You should take the ashes."

Rachel read over my shoulder. "Why'd she tell you to take the ashes?"

"She wouldn't want them if she and Mary had argued. I wonder why she helped with the funeral then."

"Maybe she was afraid you'd find something in Mary's house. 'The past is over.' That sounds like she wants you to forget about Joseph now that his mother's dead, too."

"I'd like to look at those photos again. She was really concentrating on what ones to choose, what ones to discard. But she's right. We should bury Mary's ashes and get on with our lives."

"After we find Joseph's killer." Rachel left me shivering alone by the mailbox, waiting to meet the mail truck that was just driving up the street.

15

"WHY WOULD SHE do that?" Teddy turned his back on Rachel and me. He poured himself a glass of water before he faced us again.

We were standing in his kitchen. Rachel had set her suitcase on the floor and taken off her parka. I kept mine zipped. Teddy's emotion was palpable. Something rising to the surface at the obligation to bury Mary's ashes.

Rachel took the glass from him and set it on the counter. "She wants to be with her son."

Teddy picked up the glass again and drank. He seemed more defiant than angry as he slammed the glass onto the counter. "She didn't know she was going to die. Did she think we'd call you up here for a mock burial whenever that happened. Did she even know where you live?"

Rachel took the glass again. "I always sent her a Christmas card. We were Joseph's best friends. Maybe she thought it would give us closure."

"I made my peace years ago. Bury the ashes without me." Teddy's voice was as rigid as his posture. He started out of the kitchen.

Rachel touched his arm gently to stop him. "Please, Teddy. It will only take an hour."

Teddy backed away. "And a blowtorch. The ground's frozen solid.

Come back in the spring. We'll do it then."

I wasn't sure we'd get Rachel to come back in the spring. "Name a time, Teddy," I said. "We can walk through Mary's house, take anything we want before it goes up for sale, then bury her ashes."

Rachel wrapped an arm around Teddy's waist. "We need to finish this."

"I don't want anything from Mary's house."

Rachel held him tighter. "At least meet us at the cemetery."

Teddy removed her arm. "Noon on Thursday. Then I'm done with mourning."

"Thank you." Rachel leaned into her brother and kissed his cheek.

Teddy touched his cheek, then moved his hand quickly to his side, opening and closing it into a fist. "Bury your search for Joseph's killer along with his mother's ashes. When we've finished, you can go back to New Orleans." He left us standing alone in the kitchen.

Rachel picked up her suitcase. "Come get me when you finish work tomorrow. We can go through Mary's house, and I'll stay overnight. I'll need another break from Teddy by then."

I left, welcoming the break from *both* of them.

I unlocked the door to the library then locked it behind me. The table that held three computers was empty and dusted. Seth had done his job. A dozen books that needed to be shelved were piled on the check-out desk. A sad-looking poinsettia drooped its yellow leaves beside them. I walked behind the desk to see if there was room for it in the trash Seth emptied and brought to the dump every Tuesday. The bin was only half full. I tossed in the poinsettia. The red foil wrapped around the plastic pot crackled against the edge of the can before the poinsettia came to rest, a dead plant on a grave of discarded coffee cups, candy wrappers, and dirty tissues. It reminded me to leave flowers in the snow when we buried Mary's ashes. They would die. A premature death like hers and Joseph's.

The recycle bin was filled with emptied envelopes and scraps of paper. I carried it to the computer table where I could look through it for any sign of who might have left *Deutsch Aktuell* on my desk. I took pieces out one at a time, sorting them into piles. Envelopes, advertisements, scraps with call numbers, crumpled papers with writing on them. The bin was clear, only the bottom stained from paper that sometimes was thrown in wet. I returned everything except the crumpled papers, put the bin on the floor, and sat down. One by one, I unfolded the papers and scanned the writing. A note about car safety reports that must have helped the writer decide what car to buy. A list of physical therapists in Nashua with a star next to one the writer must have chosen. The false starts of a high school paper on *The Diary of Anne Frank* that included a list of concentration camps, all misspelled. The only clue was a paper with a list of German vocabulary words. *Gift* was not one of them. Why would someone have made the list and thrown it away? I folded the paper and put it into my pocket.

An avalanche of snow slid from the roof and crashed outside the window behind the check-out counter just as I set the bin back in its place. I jumped, nearly knocking over the can filled with messy trash. My reflexes were over-active, and the library too empty, too silent, too cold. Outside, a car pulled into the parking lot. I went into my office cubicle, glad I had locked the library's door. I jumped again when whoever it was dropped a book into the return slot.

I took a deep breath and looked to see if anything had been disturbed on my desk that I hadn't noticed when Rachel and I found *Deutsch Aktuell*. The cloth that had been beside it still lay there. I picked it up to see if I recognized it as belonging to anyone I knew. It held the smell of lavender soap and looked like the cloths Seth used to clean the bathroom. I carried it to the utility cabinet. A pile of cloths were stacked on a shelf, another pile had been thrown in the bucket Seth occasionally filled to mop the floors. I took a cloth out to compare it with the one in my hand. They were identical.

The church was as empty as the library. And as cold. I listened for Seth or Pastor Pam but could hear no movement to explain why the door was unlocked. Still listening, I eased my way into the function room to see if Mary's ashes were on the table. No one was lurking there. No tables or chairs were set up. There was no evidence of the urn. The window where I remembered seeing a figure looking in at Joseph's funeral thirty years ago showed only the trunk of a maple tree that shaded the food booth we set up every August for the church fair. Beyond it I could just make out the side of the library.

I went into the kitchen. Pots that had held the soups and stews after Mary's funeral had been left to drain on the counter. Everything else had been put away. No box of photos was visible. No gray urn with a swirled design and knobless lid. Something dropped on the floor upstairs, setting off my jump reflex again. Seth must be cleaning, must have dropped a hymnal while was he dusting. But I heard no footsteps. I turned in a circle, feeling like someone in a film where the camera pans from behind onto the person about to be killed. I forced myself to walk back to the function room and look out the window I remembered too well from Joseph's funeral. A foolish gesture, but it helped rid me of the nagging sense that I was being watched.

I returned to the kitchen, opened the door to the back stairs that led to Pastor Pam's office, and flicked the light switch. No light came on, so I left the door to the kitchen open. Enough light came through the kitchen windows to let me see each step. I gripped the railing, bracing myself to confront Seth, to pretend I didn't suspect him of murder. At the top of the stairs, I pushed open the door into Pastor Pam's office. Choir robes hung ghostly white on a moveable rack. A Bible lay open the desk, its page held down with a rubber weight. Beside it, a paperweight enclosing an image of Jesus sat on a yellow legal pad. I moved the paperweight. A heavy rounded object that could have killed Joseph, except that Pastor Pam was only a toddler thirty years ago. Had she inherited the paperweight from Charles Tibbetts? I knew I was over-reacting. The paperweight wasn't our old minister's style. Not every round object was a murder weapon, I chided myself.

The scrawls on the legal pad were notes I suspected were for a sermon. It would be about the blessing of community, about how we come together in times of sorrow. I looked at the Bible passage. Matthew 15 where Jesus feeds the multitudes from seven loaves of bread. "And they all did eat and were filled." On the opposite page was one of the illustrations scattered throughout the King James Bible, this one a picture of Jesus blessing Peter's mother-in-law. Behind him stood Peter, watching. I felt again as if someone were behind *me*, watching. There was only a wall and I refused to turn and look. Instead, I moved forward into the sanctuary.

A figure sat facing me in the front pew. Seth Thompson, holding the urn. He stood, his bulk huge in the empty sanctuary, his thick glasses reflecting the colored light of a stained glass window. He raised the urn over his head as if he was going to throw it at me. I ran back into the office and picked up the telephone on Pam's desk. Seth's footsteps thudded to the side door of the chancel. If I ran downstairs, he'd follow me. The only place to hide was among the choir robes. I put down the phone, grabbed the rubber weight that held the Bible open and, hoping to mimic footsteps, threw it down the stairs, then ducked into the choir robes. The smell of incense and the candles burned on Sundays mingled with the smell of my fear.

The door opened. He went to the staircase that led to the function room. I held my breath. When he reached the bottom, I'd be able to call the police and run through the sanctuary to the front door.

He stopped half-way down, his heavy steps coming back up the stairs. He paused a moment in front of the choir robes. "You can't hide from me. Get out of there." His exaggerated dialect had turned into a voice filled with menace. He pushed the robes aside and pulled on my arm.

I managed to gasp. "Explain why you were going to throw Mary's ashes at me."

He put his hand on my back. It felt enormous as he pushed me into the sanctuary and onto a front pew. "I was just putting it on the pulpit. Stay there." The urn rested on the pulpit. He lifted it down, placed it in my lap, and sat next to me.

I could feel the heat from his body under his familiar brown jacket. It smelled as if it had been dropped into a pile of rotting leaves. I clutched the urn. I could throw it at him. He was an old man. I could out outrun him. Mary's ashes would cover her son's murderer. "You killed him," I said.

Seth bent forward, rested his head on his hands, his body tensing. He raised his head and slid along the pew away from me. "I took the book."

I took the lid off the urn, ready to throw the ashes. "Before or after you killed Joseph?"

Beneath his glasses, his eyes shot fury. "He wasn't there. Just the book tucked under the hay in a stall."

I needed to wait for him to move closer so the ashes and the urn that held them would hit him. "Why would you look there? That stall had been empty for years."

"I saw him and that girl friend of yours coming out of the barn. I went into the loft, went into all the stalls. Figured I'd find some underwear or something. I could smell the sex in the loft. It's not right. My barn's not a *brothel.*" He used the present tense as if he had forgotten that he no longer owned the barn.

"Joseph came back for the book."

"I figured that out when they told me someone killed him."

"Why didn't you give the book to the police? There was a note in it."

"In German. I saw your name. Figured *you* killed him."

"*I* didn't kill him." I looked at Mary's ashes, my heart quieting. If he was lying, he'd stick to the lie and not kill me. "Why'd you leave the book on my desk?"

"It's time for all this to be over. I'm an old man. I've held it too long. That boy's death changed my life. You didn't need to kill him." Seth stood up. He towered over me. "Take the ashes. Leave me in peace." As he walked out of the sanctuary toward the front door, he called back. "Find someone else to clean the church and the library. I quit."

I waited until I heard the door close. I put the lid back on the urn and sat alone, thinking about Seth's confession. If he had shown the book to the police, I would have become a suspect. For years he'd been living with the belief that I killed Joseph. In his way, *he* had protected *me*.

I cradled the urn in my arms, walked downstairs to the empty function room, and out the door to my car. Seth was right. The past needed to be over.

Beethoven greeted me at the door and followed me into the living room. I set the urn on the hearth without taking off my parka. I needed to walk. I needed to see Lucille. If Seth told me the truth, he didn't kill Joseph. Lucille and Hank both had stronger motives.

Beethoven approached the urn and yowled. He used his paws to try to knock off the lid. I picked him up and stroked him behind his ears until he calmed down. "It's Mary's just ashes. Like Nathan's and Cathy's next to my bed. We've got each other now." I set him on the chair that was becoming his own. He jumped off and yowled again when I picked up the urn. I carried it upstairs, Beethoven at my heels. I moved the photo of Nathan and Cathy I kept next to their urn to make room for Mary's. The two urns matched, plain and earth-toned, the color of sadness, not of resurrection.

Beethoven jumped on the bed. "Not right now." I held him close to the urn, let him smell it, then, closing my bedroom door, carried him back to his chair in front of the woodstove.

Outside the sky was clouding over, the dampness of a winter afternoon setting in. The forecast was correct. Another storm was brewing, this time winter rain that would spoil the snow and turn the landscape ugly. The white houses on Spring Hill Road were already taking on a sooty cast.

I reached Lucille's house and knocked. She took a long time to open the door. She answered it wearing a robe, the color of which matched her red-brown hair. Her hair was mussed, her face free of make-up. I stepped into her kitchen and pretended not to notice the two wine glasses empty on the counter. "I'm sorry. Were you napping?"

"I never nap. Just getting comfortable for the night. It's been a long few days, and I have a stack of papers I want to return tomorrow."

She didn't invite me to sit down. I heard a toilet flush upstairs. The stack of papers likely came wrapped in the biology teacher.

She tightened the sash of her robe. "I'd invite you for coffee but I'm on a roll into the papers. What do you need?"

"Just to tell you that I have Mary's ashes. Did you take the photos from the church?"

"I did. No one wants them now, so I burned them. I can use the magnetic board in my classroom."

My pulse quickened, pounding behind my eyes. I wanted to study the photograph of Mary and Conrad and their sons, find a clue to who had taken it, who had slipped it beside the other photos at the funeral. I could hear the fury in my voice when I managed to say through my clenched teeth, "I wouldd have taken them. Go back to your papers." Without waiting to hear more, I went outside into the raw weather, now sure that Lucille had killed Joseph.

16

BERTHA WHETMORE SAT at her usual Tuesday morning place in the library. When she had an out of wedlock child, the town had given her the job of librarian so she'd have money to raise the child. By the time Rachel and I were ten, old enough to walk alone to the library in the town hall, the town's speculations about the child's father had disappeared and, along with them, her son Joseph. Tuesdays were Bertha's library days. Ten to three when we closed and Seth Thompson drove her home. Seth rarely volunteered for anything, so I never understood his relationship with her.

Bertha unwrapped the peanut butter sandwich she ate every Tuesday in front of the sign that said No Food or Drink. If they saw her, teenagers complained that they couldn't even eat a candy bar in the library. When I suggested they sit next to Bertha and share candy, they demurred. They were right when they said she smelled. It was the smell of death, of old clothes kept in a musty trunk or hung in a closet with mothballs.

I knew her habits. She'd fold the wax paper that held her sandwich and put it into her vast pocketbook. After she ate, she'd head for the bathroom. I'd go in when she finished and wipe up a trail of urine if any hit the floor.

I was at the reference shelves checking how much space we'd pick up if we discarded our *Encyclopedia Britannica* when Bertha wended her way toward the bathroom. I shared her attachment to routine, though not to the bathroom. In high school, I always went to the *Britannica* as soon as I came into the library. I'd used it hundreds of times for reports and it felt like an old friend.

Bertha came out of the bathroom and put her pocketbook on the table where she'd been sitting. It nearly toppled her face forward onto the book she'd been reading. She straightened as much as her four and a half foot body allowed. When I motioned her to join me, she lifted her pocketbook again.

"It's okay, Bertha. I can see it from here. No one will take it."

Despite her shriveled body and her shuffling step, Bertha walked with an air of defiance, her shoulders pulled back, her head thrust forward. I thought of Elizabeth reading *Jane Eyre*. Bertha shared more than her name with the madwoman in the attic. The town may have supported her by offering a job at the library, but it never accepted her. Its kindnesses were obligations. When she reached me, she ran her hand along the shelf, then wiped the dust off of her hand and onto the black sweater she wore. If Bertha didn't smell of death, her sweater did.

"Seth should clean better." Her voice rasped the way it had after the funeral, the crackling sound of old age.

"Seth quit yesterday."

Bertha caught herself on the shelf. "'Bout time. He's nearly as old as me. Why'd you call me over?"

I wasn't sure. Nostalgia for the encyclopedias? Information that she didn't give me after the funeral? "I'm deciding whether or not to discard these encyclopedias. Do you ever see anyone using them?"

"Kids use them all the time. I have to watch that they don't mark them up. Library doesn't have enough money for me to order another set." More and more frequently, Bertha flicked into a past when kids used reference books instead of the internet, and when she was still the librarian.

"We talked about Joseph Wheeler on Saturday. He used to come to the library with me. Do you remember him?"

"Joseph was a good boy." Behind her granny glasses, Bertha's eyes glazed over. "He left. Gone to Cal-a-fon-ia or somewhere. Keep these encyclopedias. Kids use them all the time."

Bertha thrust her head forward and shuffled back to her table. She sat down and picked up the book she was reading. Edith Wharton's *Summer*. "Joseph was a good boy. His father took him away."

His father? Was Bertha confused? Could Seth Thompson be Joseph Whetmore's father? Was that why he drove the boy to the bus terminal in Nashua? Why he volunteered to help an old woman? Was he the lover of this woman ten years his senior?

"I'm glad you tagged the kitchen table." Rachel blew on a spoonful of the lobster stew we were splitting for dinner. It wasn't the celebration we'd promised ourselves if we found Joseph's murderer, but we needed something to soothe the exhaustion that had invaded us while we claimed some of Mary's things for ourselves. We spent the late afternoon walking through her house, knowing we were looking for a clue to Joseph's death more than claiming anything that had been hers. In the end, Rachel took only the pewter and pink glass candy dish we coveted as kids. I filled a box with some kitchen things, a few books, and the photographs Lucille and I hadn't chosen for Mary's funeral. I'd go through them again and keep the good ones.

"I feel a little guilty about tagging the table. I should buy it when there's an estate sale."

"You know that's ridiculous. There'll be plenty of money to endow a scholarship."

I sat facing the statue of the Gloucester fisherman at the entryway to Clive's Chowder House, noticing whoever came in the front door. A petite woman pulled a hat off to reveal short hair, almost silver and no longer highlighted with a streak of color. Susan Warner. She began highlighting her hair with a small streak of lavender or maroon or copper when she retired. After she had solved her third murder, she gave up on the color, claiming that it brought misery not independence from an uptight administration at Souhegan College. She stopped at the take-out counter.

"Wait here." I slipped out of the booth and approached her. "Susan." I'd long ago dropped the Mrs. Warner. "Want to join us?" I gestured toward Rachel.

Susan knew the town of Shelby. Graniteville kids attended our high school until the town built its own in the late nineties. Her daughter Erika was still in Graniteville's elementary school when Joseph was killed, but Susan would remember the murder even if she didn't know him.

She followed my gesture. "I won't interrupt?"

"Not at all. In fact, we could use your help."

She slid into the booth next to me and I introduced her to Rachel. "Rachel's Ted Cummings' sister. She came for Mary Wheeler's funeral."

Susan opened her to-go bag and took out a plastic container of chowder. "I was sorry to hear that she died. Erika took piano lessons from her."

"Where's Erika now?" I never knew Erika, but I knew she'd helped solve the murders Susan found herself immersed in.

"Married and living in New Orleans."

Rachel stopped her spoon half-way to her mouth. "Where in New Orleans? That's where I live."

"Neron Place. At the end of the trolley line. She's a nurse at Ochsner Hospital. Her husband's a geologist she met when we were on a bicycle trip on The Natchez Trace."

Susan gave me a perfect opening for what I wanted to ask. "Isn't that when someone was murdered?"

Susan sprinkled oyster crackers into her chowder. "At least one thing good came out of it. You should look her up, Rachel."

"I will." Rachel took her cell phone out of the Baggalini she used as a purse. "What's her phone number?"

"504-555-2560. She'll like hearing from someone who went to Shelby High School."

I set down my spoon. I wanted information, not the lobster stew that, even split with Rachel, was making me feel stuffed. "That's what I want to ask about. Do you remember when Joseph Wheeler was killed?"

"In that barn with the cow's head, right?"

Rachel reached both her hands onto her head as if she were envisioning the cow. For months after the murder, we both imagined the cow watching what happened. "We were the ones who found him there."

I touched my hair to remind Rachel not to give in to the habit of twisting strands of her own. She moved her hands back to the table and spooned a hunk of lobster into her mouth. "Did people from Graniteville ever guess at who could have killed Joseph?"

Susan set down her spoon. "Oh, yes. Our teenagers were still going to your school. After a time, they stopped. I don't see what help I can be. I'm done with murders."

"Rachel and I went off to college and the case went cold," I said.

Susan wiped a spot of chowder off the table. "Jog my memory. How was he killed? Why are you looking into it now?"

I looked at Rachel, wondering how much she was willing to share with a woman she didn't know. Susan had become a celebrity of sorts when she'd solved a murder in Graniteville, but Rachel didn't know that. Unless Teddy told her, she knew only what I'd just said about a murder on The Natchez Trace.

Rachel spun her spoon around. It sounded loud against the Formica table. "Someone hit him on the head. I've been dreaming about it for months. When Teddy told me that Mary died, I knew I had to come back, put my ghosts to rest."

Susan watched Rachel fiddling with her spoon. "Do you know why you started to dream about it?"

Rachel hesitated before she shared a part of the story she hadn't told me. "It started when I read 'Barn Burning.'"

"Faulkner," said Susan. "But the barn's still standing."

"Doesn't matter. That's when the dreams started."

When it became obvious Rachel had said all she wanted to, Susan directed her question to me. "Do you have suspects?"

Rachel continued to fiddle with her spoon as she named Seth Thompson.

Susan pulled her head back in surprise. "Even thirty years ago Seth was crotchety, but I've never thought of him as a murderer."

Despite what I'd told Rachel about Seth taking the German book, she couldn't let go of her suspicion. "He hated that teenagers kept partying at his barn."

Susan dipped a piece of bread into her chowder. "Was Joseph Wheeler a partier? I never knew him."

Rachel defended Joseph. "He was my boyfriend. He didn't party."

"Anyone else you think might have killed him?" Susan stopped eating and listened.

Rachel and I told her about Joseph going to the barn, about his suspicions of Hank Huckabay's side business, and about Hank's ball peen hammer. We confessed that Rachel had been with Joseph in the barn, and that I had left the German book that Seth found. We left out the part about sex and Rachel's pregnancy.

"I think Seth is unlikely," said Susan. "Maybe Hank. I stopped buying gas from him years ago. He deserves the name Hank the Crank. I'm not surprised he has an illegal side business. Is that it?

Just two male suspects?" She took another bite of chowder.

"There's something else about Seth," I said. "Rachel, I didn't tell you this, but Bertha Whetmore was in the library this morning and we talked about him."

Susan closed up her chowder container. "I used to take Erika to your library. Bertha was old even then."

"She had a child named Joseph." I looked toward the door where a tall, heavy man came in. Paul the Pole, the boy Rachel told me was with Teddy at Skip's the night Joseph died. He'd gained about fifty pounds and grown a beard. I had seen him around Shelby now and again, one of the ones who never left. He stood at the take-out counter now, his back to us. I willed him not to turn. If he saw us, he'd recognize Rachel and start interrogating her.

"You know the rumors about Bertha and Seth?" Susan put the chowder container into her to-go bag.

I spoke as much to Rachel as to Susan. "I guessed this morning. Seth Thompson is her child's father."

Rachel squeezed my leg. "Seth had a son he never acknowledged? Bertha must know how awful he is, then. She might even know that he killed Joseph."

I touched her hand on my leg. It was as cold as our case. "Bertha gets confused. Seth drops her at the library every Tuesday when he picks up the trash for the dump. I never understood why. Maybe guilt about abandoning her with a child. But he's not guilty of Joseph's murder."

"Don't be so sure. Isn't he a lot younger than Bertha?" said Rachel.

"Like Lucille Larcom and Eric Donaldson. Lucille's another suspect." I told Susan about how Lucille signed Joseph's memorial page, about how *gift* could mean *poison*, about how we thought she might have been sleeping with Eric when he was still in high school, and that Joseph might have known about it.

Susan looked toward Paul, who was flirting with the young girl filling his order. "I didn't know Eric Donaldson, but I know Lucille. There was a lot of talk about them when they married."

"Talk?" I said

"About a teacher marrying a former student."

"Does that happen often?" I watched Paul lean against the counter, closer to the girl than he needed to be.

"It's endemic in colleges. Mostly male professors and female students. Not so much in high schools."

"Were there rumors that Eric and Lucille were sleeping together when he was still in high school?" I asked.

"I have no idea," said Susan. "People talk. They love drama."

I pushed away my chowder bowl, leaving a last bite of lobster. Paul took the to-go bag from the girl, letting his hand brush hers. "Was there talk about who might have killed Joseph?"

"Plenty. But I don't remember much. Just that maybe another teenager killed him."

Paul walked to the fisherman's statue, stopped and came toward us. He stood beside our table looking down at Rachel. "Rachel Cummings. Cleopatra Rachel. Come to find a murderer, have you?"

Rachel jumped from the booth and pushed against his beer belly. "You saw Joseph that night. You *know* something."

"Just that you're back and bringing up the past. Leave it. That boyfriend of yours is history."

He pivoted away from us and left, leaving me with the fear that the long-ago rumors about a teenage killer might be right.

As we drove, we went over what Susan had told us, the radio playing Stravinsky's *Rite of Spring* in the background. Two older woman/younger man romances. Lucille and Eric. Bertha and Seth. There was no connection between them. All we could imagine was that Joseph knew about them both. Rachel couldn't let go of Seth.

"Seth is a bigot and a bastard, but I don't think he's a murderer. What about what Susan said? Another teenager killed Joseph?"

"Paul the Pole? He was with us that night at Skip's."

The surging strings in the death dance of Stravinsky's final movement led us into Teddy's driveway. "Go inside. Get some sleep. I'll pick you up when I finish work tomorrow. We can think more about Paul then."

"I like the idea of another sleepover. Maybe we can feel like kids the way we did yesterday."

When she got out of the car, she dropped Mary's candy dish. I jumped out after her, fearing the dish—like our pasts—had shattered. I stooped to pick it up while Rachel stood motionless above me. The lid had fallen off and lay unbroken on the ground. I stood and placed the lid back on the dish. "There's just a tiny crack on the side." Like the crack in *The Golden Bowl*. Like our relationship. Cracked by absence.

Rachel took the dish from me, murmured thank you. Without looking back, she climbed the porch steps and went into the house.

17

THE STORM CAME in at midnight. Heavy rain, and wind that penetrated the rattling windows. If the temperature dropped and there was snow that hadn't been washed from the roof, there'd be ice dams and leaks. I forced myself out of bed to check the spare room that leaked two years ago. It was empty except for suitcases and a chest where I stored what few things I had from Nathan and Cathy. My husband's college diploma, my daughter's favorite stuffed giraffe. Things only I cared about. A rocking chair I'd used when I nursed Cathy sat on a bare wood floor whose wrought iron nails declared its age. Mary's piano would fill the emptiness of what I named my mourning room.

I felt around the window where I'd had the leak. It was dry, the repairs holding. I jumped when the last of the snow on the roof plunged next to the spot where Rachel and I made snow angels. There'd be only a soggy pile of snow and dirt in the morning.

On my way to the stairs, I glanced into my bedroom at Beethoven sleeping. He'd sniffed at Mary's urn once more when I let him back into the room. Cats might have nine lives but they didn't seem to have long memories. The ceiling and walls all looked dry. Outside the kitchen window, water gushed from the storm drain on the back side of the house. I turned on the side light and could just make out the puddles catching the dirt that the rain was washing from my car. The world would look sad in the morning, but at least my car would be clean. Dim headlights came slowly down the road, plowing through a waterfall of rain and stopping at my driveway. I turned off the outside light, checked the lock on my door, and went into the hallway to check the front door lock. The headlights moved again. A driver being cautious in the rain, I told myself.

I started toward the cellar. There'd be a puddle that formed every storm when rain seeped through the granite boulders that served as the foundation. My feet were bare and freezing. It could wait until morning. I went back to my bedroom, crawled under the covers, and warmed my feet under Beethoven. He stretched, then settled back in the same position, his body comforting me as I willed myself back to sleep.

Dreams kept startling me awake. Bertha holding a baby. Joseph lying with Paul the Pole standing over him. Nathan driving a car past my house, Cathy in the back seat crying for him to stop. I woke to the comfort of my last dream, in which Rachel and I were making snow angels in Teddy's field. Beethoven stretched and jumped off the bed. I opened my eyes to dreary daylight.

The sky outside my bedroom window was encased in fog. The rain hadn't cleansed Shelby, and the day promised raw weather. I rummaged through a drawer in my armoire for pants and a warm sweater. I dressed in the way I'd perfected for the cold of a bedroom the heat never warmed enough. Socks on first, pants on before I took off my warm bathrobe, a quick fastening of my bra and my sweater pulled over it, then a fluffing of my hair that got more gray than brown with every passing year. I timed myself once. Four minutes and I was brushing my teeth and putting in contact lenses. Three more and I was downstairs stoking the woodstove. Today, I paused in front of my mirror. The gold of my sweater was a good color for me. My fall complexion pointed me to muted yellows and oranges and reds, colors of the turning leaves in October. Next to Rachel,

I felt not exactly dowdy, but boring, classic to her artistic. Even in high school, I'd envied her air of sophistication. Today, I was slower. The dreariness of the morning turned my envy to sympathy. I'd accepted a sorrow that never fully healed while she'd let hers fester until it invaded her art work. I was tired of her obsession, ready to bury Mary's ashes and to move on. I had no energy to add Paul Sanderson or anyone else who had been a classmate to the list.

Downstairs, I put three logs on the woodstove before I went into the kitchen to fix coffee and toast with the bread I'd bought at The Village Store after I dropped Rachel at Teddy's. I sat for a long time dawdling over my coffee at the kitchen table, picturing how Mary's table would look in its place. It would keep her memory alive even after my grief at her death had faded.

Beethoven found me in the kitchen and meowed for food. "You ate already, but have some more. Maybe it will make you forget that I closed my bedroom door. No yowling at Mary's ashes."

I filled his bowl then went upstairs to brush my teeth again. The bathroom mirror told me I looked tired. Walking to the library would at least give my face some color. I went down the stairs to the living room, checked the fire, and got my parka from the hook above the stove. At the top of the cellar stairs, I found the rubber boots that would keep my feet dry while I walked to the library.

Picking up an envelope with a check I needed to mail and armed for the raw weather, I went outside. It was the kind of day that made me wonder why I stayed in New Hampshire. Damp, cold, the snow covered in dirt and fallen twigs. I dodged puddles that had settled into the ruts in my driveway. Every summer I raked gravel to smooth them over, and every spring frost heaves formed them again. Before I opened my mailbox, I raised the flag to signal to the carrier that there was mail to pick up. I held my breath as I pulled open the cover. Empty. Lucille hadn't left another note.

When I moved away from the mailbox, I nearly tripped on

something wedged into the dwindling snowbank Andy had left when he shoveled out the mailbox. Whatever it was, it had too much white under a coating of dirt to be a rock. I bent and picked it up. A baseball. No markings. Just a plain ball whose stitching was starting to unravel. I remembered the slowing headlights I saw through the curtain of rain in the night. Why would someone throw a baseball out a car window in the middle of winter? I convinced myself that it wasn't threatening, that Andy had dropped it when he was shoveling. Eleven-year-old boys kept all kinds of things as lucky charms.

I threw the baseball back in the snowbank and started toward town. At the edge of her driveway, I saw Lucille looking out her kitchen window. I glanced at my watch. 9:07. She should have been at the school already. Maybe she was sick. Maybe her car wouldn't start after all the rain. If Rachel were with me, she'd say to stop, ask if anything was wrong, confront her about Mary's will. I could do that much, but I wasn't sure I could ask her the important question, if she was sleeping with Eric when he was still in high school.

Lucille opened her door when I knocked. She was dressed for teaching. Corduroy pants, a V-neck sweater whose V was cut just a little too low, her bare neck accented with an emerald pendant, the color of which matched her sweater. "I saw you walking. That was some storm last night. Everything okay at your house?" Her shrill voice sounded more friendly than it did the other day when I interrupted what I was sure was an affair with the biology teacher.

"No problem. Is something wrong at school? I thought you'd be there."

"Delayed opening. Apparently there was a leak into one of the classrooms. They're cleaning up and making sure there's no damage to the roof. Safety first for our dear teenagers."

"I thought you liked them." *Too* much, I said to myself.

"I do. But I'm always happy for a few hours' reprieve. I was just

157

about to pour myself a second cup of coffee. Join me?" She glanced at the wood-framed clock on her kitchen wall. She once told me that it had hung in the office of the man who owned the mill where her ancestor Lucy Larcom had worked. Unlike the fashionable clothes she wore, everything in Lucille's house was nineteenth-century accurate. A kitchen table made from one where the mill girls worked making cotton. Three chairs, all different, two from a boarding house where the mill girls had lived. She motioned me to the chair she claimed Lucy Larcom sat in when she'd been promoted to bookkeeper at the Boott mills. I doubted the story was true.

I ran my hand over the table. "Thanks, but I'm on my way to the library. Did I ever tell you how much I like this table?"

"Every time you sit at it."

I found my opening. "Mary's will said that Rachel, Teddy, and I should take anything we want before there's an estate sale. I'm taking her kitchen table."

"Nice that she kept you in her will."

I needed to be careful that I didn't reveal what Holly let slip out. "Did she leave you something?"

"No." Lucille poured coffee into one of her collection of hand painted mugs. They were unusual. Heavy pottery rounded to a flat bottom, with no designs, just in different colors of the earth. Like her clothes, her dishes weren't nineteenth century.

"I'm surprised. You were close."

"*Were*. She cut off our friendship months ago."

I moved away from the table. "But you were so good helping with her funeral."

Lucille held tight to her cup when she sat down. "Needed to pretend nothing was wrong. Half the school was watching me, thinking we were the best of friends."

I couldn't leave now that she was talking about Mary, so I sat at the table, motioning her not to get up to pour me coffee. "What happened?"

"She imagined something about me and Eric. Thought Joseph knew it and that's why he got killed. I know you and Rachel are bringing up that time. Forget Joseph."

That phrase again. If she were here, Rachel would have blurted out that Joseph knew she was sleeping with Eric. I couldn't be so blunt about something we didn't know for sure. "If you tell me what Mary found out, maybe it'll help us find Joseph's murderer."

She clunked her coffee cup on the table and stood to face me. "It's ancient history. If you're looking for who killed Joseph, cross me off the list. I had no motive."

I pushed my chair away from the table and backed to the kitchen door away from the coffee mug Lucille was holding like a weapon. "Why would I think you killed him?"

"Don't be coy. Eric was a mistake, but we were both young. When we married, I thought it would make everything okay. It didn't."

I found the door knob. "What did Mary think?"

Lucille dumped what was left of her coffee in the sink and put down the mug. "She saw Eric's father at a conference somewhere. When she mentioned my name... Never mind what Conrad said. He hates me."

"Hates you because you slept with his teenaged son, or because you ended his relationship with Mary? Or both?"

"Don't make assumptions. I didn't end his relationship. Joseph's murder did. Which I *didn't* commit."

I gripped the doorknob. "Joseph knew. That's why you wrote 'gift' in the yearbook. He was poison to you if he told."

Lucille grabbed her coffee cup. I thought she was going to throw it at me. "Leave it, Deborah. I didn't kill Joseph. Go to your stupid job at that podunk library. Enough's enough. The past is over."

She waited for me to leave, then slammed the door shut. She'd confessed nothing, but had denied a murder I never said she'd committed.

A car passed me, unleashing a spray of dirty water onto my pants. "Slow down!" I yelled into the air just as I saw Andy Carkin walking toward me, swinging a bag.

I calmed myself to talk with him. "Didn't sleep in because of the late start to school?"

"Couldn't. I lost my lucky baseball. Thought I might have left it at The Village Store."

"You dropped it by my mailbox. It's still there on top of what little is left of the snowbank."

Andy did a quick hop in the air. "Thank you. I always carry that ball. My dad gave it to me. It's the one he used for the winning pitch when the Shelby Cavaliers won the championship."

I remembered that year but not that Andy's father had been on the team. They played all season in memory of Joseph. I needed to stop thinking of teenage murderers. "I'm glad I saw your ball."

"It's going to help me make the team when I get to high school." Andy broke into a run, and I quickened my pace to the library.

The weather was as raw as my thoughts. Two of our three suspects denied that they murdered Joseph. I believed them, but I knew that Rachel would say I believed people too easily. She was right. For the last thirty years, I believed she wasn't in the barn with Joseph. Another teenager. *Nonsense*, I told myself. I concentrated on Hank Huckabay.

As if in response, I saw Hank at Seth's side door, his arm searching for the empty sleeve of his jacket. He saw me and watched until I walked past. I reached the church, convinced that he and Seth had been talking about Joseph's murder, and that Hank was following me to tell me to forget Joseph. Thirty years ago, Hank had kept Seth's tractor running. Perhaps he knew that Seth killed Joseph, helped him to hide whatever weapon he'd used. Or the other way around. Seth had seen Hank leaving the barn the night of Joseph's murder. I knew I was over-reacting. But someone who lived in town thirty years ago had killed Joseph, and was now warning Rachel and me not to dig up the past.

Whoever was following me was coming closer. I fumbled in my pocket for the library key. If it was Hank, I'd lock myself inside until Jody arrived for the library opening at ten o'clock. At the ramp, I turned to look. It was Irwin Trombly minus Rufus. Irwin hadn't even lived in town when Joseph was murdered, but when he came up the ramp toward me, I clutched the key the way I'd learned in a women's self-defense class.

I took the book he handed me, relaxing my hand on the key. He was only returning a library book. "Where's Rufus?" I wanted to be pleasant but not friendly enough to encourage a relationship.

"Sleeping in his dog bed and staying out of this raw weather. I'm surprised you didn't drive to work."

"I should have, but it's supposed to warm up later. I need the exercise."

His eyes moved up and down my body. "I like how you stay fit."

The comment carried the innuendo I heard too often in his voice. I unlocked the door. "Thanks for returning the book." I closed the door behind me and locked it. Still holding the key, I walked around the shelves, looked upstairs in the children's area, checked the bathroom, then settled myself in my cubicle. I picked up the phone to call Rachel. Teddy answered, his hello muffled. "Can I talk with Rachel?"

His voice became clearer. "She and Janet took Elizabeth to school. They haven't come back yet. Must have stopped for coffee or something."

"Tell her I'll come around four. And, Teddy, thanks for agreeing to meet us at the cemetery tomorrow. It means a lot to Rachel."

"So she says." With that, he hung up.

~ ~ ~ ~ ~ ~ ~

Holly Hoche's voice entered the library before she did. I looked up from the computer table where I was helping Grace Mason, the only girl in town I knew who was being homeschooled. Her mother dropped her off every Wednesday, expecting Grace to research whatever she'd been assigned. Every Wednesday, I ended up helping Grace navigate to a suitable online site. Today she was working on Judas Iscariot and writing a paper about his betrayal of Christ. Mostly she was copying sentences from Wikipedia and I was trying to show her note-taking techniques that would help her avoid plagiarism.

I left Grace to her note-taking and approached Holly, who was guiding Bertha Whetmore into a room warm enough to fog her granny glasses. "She sits at that table," I said to Holly, who was helping Bertha take off the same black coat that blanketed her frail body well into spring. I hung the coat on the rack next to the door. I put Bertha's gloves into the black hat with ear flaps she'd worn every winter I could remember, and perched these on top of the coat. They smelled of moth balls and foggy air.

Bertha stopped by Grace and asked in her cracking voice, "What are you looking up on that machine?"

Without looking away from the screen, Grace mumbled, "Judas."

Bertha went to the stacks where a day ago I'd been debating about whether to discard the *Britannica*. Holly was jangling her keys, anxious to leave. "What's she doing here on a Wednesday?" I asked.

"I was at her house. She needed to sign a new will."

"Another new will? Why Bertha this time?"

"You'll have to ask her. She's a little confused today, but we went over the changes she should have made almost a year ago when we confirmed that her son had died."

"He died? How?" Was that why Bertha wrote, "He murdered both of you"?

"I have no idea. It was only last year that we were able to confirm that he died a dozen years ago, and is buried in Montana. Bertha insisted on a memorial service. The only people there were ones who remembered him. All old-timers except for me."

"Was Seth Thompson there?" I watched as Bertha emerged from the stacks balancing two encyclopedias along with her pocketbook. They likely weighed as much as she did. She set the encyclopedias next to Grace, who ignored her.

"Probably. She mentioned Seth this morning. Said something about how he won't get her money. But like I said, she's confused today. Why are you asking about him?"

I listened to Bertha trying to explain to Grace how to find Judas in the encyclopedia. The raspy cracking of her voice carried through the nearly empty library. "Just follow the alphabet until you get to the J's. You can use this index to find if there's material on Joseph in any other encyclopedia."

Grace pushed the encyclopedias away. "I'm working on Judas, not Joseph. Leave me alone. I know what I'm doing."

Bertha tried to stand erect, but she looked more defeated than defiant when she moved to the table she claimed as her own. Grace's homeschooling apparently didn't include lessons in manners.

"Will you come back to get Bertha?" I left Holly's question about Seth unanswered.

"I was hoping you might take her home."

"I walked. As long as Jody's here, I suppose I can walk home and come back with my car."

Holly glanced at her watch. "Never mind. My last appointment's at two o'clock. You close at three, right?"

"Yes."

"I should just make it." Holly left without saying goodbye to

Bertha, who was sitting with nothing in front of her except her pocketbook. I sat down next to her. "Would you like me to get you a book?"

Bertha opened her pocketbook and took out her sandwich and the library's copy of *Summer*. "Still reading this one."

The book's cover was stained with something that looked like chocolate. When Bertha opened it to her bookmark, there were more stains. I'd have to throw away the Library of America's copy of Wharton's novel and order a new one. It was the third time since Christmas that Bertha had spilled food on a library book. I knew I'd have to say something eventually, or direct her to the shelf of free books that people donated. She wouldn't like them. Bertha was old, she was confused, but she liked to read the classics, not the romance or mystery novels people tended to leave.

I felt awkward looking down at her, so I sat. Grace was doing okay on her own, and the new books I was ordering on patrons' recommendations could wait. I thought about the blurb for Clive Rosengren's novels. I could really use his PI Eddie Collins right now to find a thread in whatever Bertha had said about Seth Thompson. *If* Seth was the killer, which I still doubted.

"It's nice to see you here on a Wednesday," I said.

Bertha lifted her head. "Wednesday? That's my appointment day."

"Your appointment was with Holly. Now you get to hang out in the library. She'll pick you up when we close."

"Seth's not coming?"

"No."

"He never was reliable. Left me before Joseph was born. Took him from me. No better than a murderer. I left it to you."

I searched for a thread of logic in Bertha's free association. Was she suggesting that she was leaving it to me to prove that Seth killed Joseph? "A murderer? Do you remember the other Joseph?

The one murdered in Seth's barn?"

"Course I do. My Joseph was gone. He's dead, you know. Seth killed him sure as that boy in his barn."

Bertha's hand trembled on *Summer*. I folded my hand over hers. The skin felt as thin as tracing paper. "Are you saying that Seth killed Joseph Wheeler? In his barn?"

She pulled her hand away. Beneath her glasses, her eyes held the hazy cast of old age and confusion. "How would I know? Seth took my Joseph away. Good as killed him." Bertha bent to her book and began mumbling Wharton's words out loud.

I spoke over her reading. "I don't understand. If Seth killed Joseph, why do you let him bring you to the library?" I left the Josephs ambiguous to see where it would lead her. Seth hadn't killed her son. He'd just never acknowledged him even after he helped him to run away.

"Like to watch him feel guilty. He won't get my money. What I told that Hollyhock person. I left it to you."

"Left *what* to me?" As far as I knew, Bertha lived on a tiny pension in a house that must have belonged to her parents. Once a year, people from the church made repairs and made sure she stayed safe in it. Showed her a kindness, as she liked to say.

"Not to you. To the library. Leave me alone now. Go show that girl how to use an encyclopedia. Joseph will help her when he gets here. He always likes to help the pretty girls." She bent to her book again, lost in the past and leaving me to wonder if she was confused about Seth, or if all these years, she knew he was a murderer.

18

I LOCKED THE door to the library and followed Holly and Bertha down the ramp to Holly's car. Covered in her black coat and hat, Bertha looked like a shadow in the lowering light of a January afternoon. I helped her into the car, this elderly woman who once had enough passion to conceive a child out of wedlock, and enough strength to raise him alone. Though she wore no scarlet A, she spent her life in a town that both pitied and judged her.

Before I closed the door, I settled her pocketbook on her lap. "This is too heavy," I said. "Would you like me to help you pick out a lighter one?"

She grabbed the handle as if I were trying to steal it. "I'm used to it." She kept hold of it as Holly reached over to help her buckle her seat belt.

"I'll see you on Tuesday." I closed the car door. Bertha was like me, a survivor of sorrow who found refuge among library books.

A deepening, drier cold replaced the raw air of the morning as I walked past the church, past Seth's where an outside light and an empty driveway signaled that he wasn't home. I went into The Village Store to buy a pork loin, some of its extra sharp cheddar from Vermont, and a bottle of wine for dinner. I'd serve Rachel applesauce and mac and cheese as a side to the pork. The store's vegetables were rarely good in the winter, but its meat was okay, and

166

its cheese was as sharp and tangy as the cheddar Teddy stocked at his farm stand in summer. The store was the same size it had been when Rachel and I used to stop on our bicycles to buy ice cream sandwiches. Four short aisles crowded with the most basic of foods and household items. However, the side wall held a surprisingly good selection of wine.

I picked up a basket at the door. The large front window was left clear of products, so what little light remained of the day seeped in. Overhead lights made the inside look inviting. I went first to the wall of wine. I was holding a bottle of pinot noir when someone came up behind me and said "Deborah." I jumped, nearly dropping the bottle. Hank Huckabay. I faced him, then stepped back a few inches.

"Wine and cigarettes? Don't let that friend of yours corrupt you."

I took three more steps backwards. "Just wine for dinner. Who's minding your cigarette operation?"

Again, he closed the space between us. He reminded me of a bulldog. His eyes shot hatred. "My sales, you mean? Got me another teenager to work after school."

I backed away again. "Another?"

"Yuh, another."

I walked away from him, hoping he wouldn't follow me to the meat counter. Irwin was there with a ten-pound bag of dog food in one hand and a package of hamburger in the other. "Something wrong, Deborah? You look upset."

"I'm fine. Just tired."

He glanced over my shoulder. "There's Hank the Crank. He was asking me about the friend you introduced me to the other day."

That surprised me. Irwin didn't know Rachel. "Why would he ask you?"

He set his hamburger back in the meat cooler and repositioned the bag of dog food before he picked it up again. "That's what I asked him. He said something about a murder I never heard of. Is he bothering you? Want me to drive you home?"

"Thanks, but I'll be okay. Hank's leaving now." I saw him at the counter paying for a six-pack of Budweiser.

"If he bothers you, just give me a call. I hate buying gas from him, but I was almost on empty when I saw you."

He touched my hand that was holding the shopping basket. The touch was light, warm and inviting. Still, I wasn't interested. Without answering, I looked in the meat compartment and chose the largest pork loin. After I saw Irwin pay and leave the store, I went to the checkout counter and ordered a pound of cheddar from the wheel next to the register.

"You're my best cheese customer," said Kay, the woman who bought the store when Rachel and I were in elementary school. She was approaching seventy now, and I knew she wanted to sell it. I hoped whoever bought the store would keep it stocked with the quality items Kay ordered to mix in with the popular Fruit Loops and Pringles. While she wrapped the cheese and put my meager purchases in a paper bag, I stood next to the ice cream freezer. Before she rang up my bill, I opened the freezer and took out two ice cream sandwiches.

She laughed when I handed them to her. "I heard your friend was back in town. Rachel? I remember when you two were kids riding your bikes and buying ice cream sandwiches. You were close. It's nice that she came back for Mary's funeral."

That information had traveled to every corner of town.

Janet opened the door before I knocked. "Rachel went upstairs for something when she saw your car. Said she'll be right down."

Janet had been baking and must have touched her hair. Its coarse black was streaked with flour on one side. I wanted to brush it off, but was afraid to offend her. We were friendly but not friends. Teddy created some kind of barrier between us. He told me once that I reminded him of Rachel, who'd abandoned him, and Joseph, who'd died. Whether or not he confided any of that to Janet, she avoided getting too close to me.

"You must be baking. It smells wonderful."

Janet wiped a floury hand on her pants. "Apple pie. I still have bushels of apples in our cellar. Want some?"

"I'd love some."

"Go talk with Teddy while I get them." She reached between her refrigerator and counter for one of the paper bags she stored there. I watched the white patch of flour on the back of her jeans as she opened the door to the cellar. I knew that baking relaxed her. This week, she must have been doing it to relieve some of the tension between Teddy and Rachel that was palpable in the house.

Teddy stood in front of the bookcase that held the cannonball bookends and the photo of Joseph and him. When I came in, he went to his chair and opened what I saw was a seed catalog.

"Ordering for spring?" I asked.

"Just getting ideas. I buy seeds in bulk at Orde's supply store. Seed potatoes, corn, beans, beets. All the usual stuff."

"Anything exotic in there you want to try? Okra or something?"

"In New Hampshire? You're kidding. I planted collard greens last year and couldn't *give* them away." Teddy closed the seed catalog and stood up to help Rachel who was coming downstairs with her suitcase and one of my canvas bags.

I heard Janet coming back up the cellar stairs, and then taking the pie out of the oven. The smell of apple and cinnamon and pastry crust drifted into the living room. Rachel called into the kitchen. "Come in here, Janet. We have something for you."

Janet came in, pot holders still in her hands.

Rachel glanced out the window. "Will Elizabeth be home soon?

We picked out something for each of you at Mary's yesterday. I waited for Deb to come because we chose the things together."

Teddy stiffened. "If I wanted anything, I'd have come with you."

"You should have something." Rachel looked at her watch. "How long will we have to wait for Elizabeth?"

"She's at volleyball practice, then she's walking to her piano lesson." Janet lay the potholders on the shelf next to the cannonball bookends.

"She'll like this." Rachel picked up the bag she'd set on the floor and took out a metronome. She went through the door into the room they'd christened the music room. It held an upright piano, Teddy's three guitars, and a violin I'd never heard Janet play. Still holding the bag, Rachel came back into the room.

"It's perfect," said Janet. "Elizabeth loved Mary. She's not sure about this new teacher."

"There's still lots of music at Mary's if Elizabeth wants to raid it." Rachel reached into the bag again. She handed Janet a handmade storage box for scissors and needle and thread. "We put your name on Mary's sewing machine. I know your quilts are all hand sewn, and I'm guessing you have a sewing machine, but maybe you can find use for a second one. Hers is one of those black models embossed in some gold-colored metal. If you want it, Teddy can pick it up in his truck."

Janet rubbed her hand over the box. "This box is beautiful. And old. Mary told me it belonged to her grandmother. Her sewing machine is over a hundred years old, but it's better than mine. Teddy, maybe you can get it tomorrow after you go to the cemetery."

Teddy stood unmoving in front of us, saying nothing.

Rachel took the last item out of her bag. A dozen of the comic books Joseph collected. "We found them tucked into a box at the back of the closet in Joseph's room. There are lots more if you want to get them tomorrow when you get the sewing machine."

Teddy took the comic books and, without saying anything, left the room. We heard him climb the stairs, heard him banging in his and Janet's bedroom.

I took the empty bag from Rachel. "We didn't mean to upset him."

"Too many memories right now. Vintage comic books are worth as much as old baseball cards. He'll probably sell them. Except for that photo," she pointed to the bookcase, "he hates to be reminded of Joseph. He'll be okay eventually."

"Eventually, when I leave," said Rachel. "Let's go, Deb. Teddy can lick his wounds in private."

The pinot noir didn't go with the ice cream sandwiches, but we toasted with the few sips remaining in each of our glasses before we took our first bite of the cookie-covered ice cream.

"They're not as good as I remember." I swallowed the last of my wine and set the glass on the table.

"Things never are." Rachel copied me with her wine. "Maybe they'd taste better with coffee."

I found a plate, put the two sandwiches in the freezer, and started the coffee maker. Its loud grinding made Beethoven jump away from the dish where he was eating.

"You're good in the kitchen," said Rachel when I sat back down. "I wouldn't have thought to make apple sauce in the microwave with those apples Janet gave you."

"I'm queen of the microwave. Living alone doesn't give me much chance to cook anything fancy."

"I'm queen of Annie's mac and cheese."

"I confess to always having a box on hand." The coffee aroma started to fill the kitchen.

Rachel ran her hand over my table. "What will you do with this one when you get Mary's? It's a nice table."

"I'll put it upstairs in my mourning room along with the piano."

"Mourning room?"

I explained how I named the room, and how I often sat in the rocking chair thinking of Nathan and Cathy.

"You should let go."

"I have. I remember our happy times more than I cry at their loss. You need to let go of Joseph." The coffee pot beeped. I stopped where the conversation was headed by getting up to pour it. Pushing away an image of Lucille's heavy mugs with the rounded bottoms perfectly calibrated so they wouldn't tip over, I took the ice cream sandwiches from the freezer.

I bit into the sandwich and washed it down with the steaming coffee. "Much better combination."

"Agreed," said Rachel. "Coffee's good. Strong and black."

"Teddy still like it this way?"

"We learned to drink it when we fed our father cups to help him get over his hangovers."

"I never realized how hard those years were for you. I should have been a better friend."

"You were good enough."

I listened to the sleet that had started outside. I could see the tiny crystals landing on my car. My windshield would be covered with ice in the morning. So would Joseph's grave unless the sun came out early enough to soften the ground. "Snow, mud, ice. No wonder you left New England."

Rachel dropped a piece of the cookie part of her ice cream sandwich into her coffee. She fished it out with a finger and put it into her mouth. "I won't come back again."

"Not even to visit?"

"I'm making Teddy nervous. He can visit me in New Orleans. He does sometimes, you know. The memories aren't so strong there.

We can feel like brother and sister again."

"It's because you're here after Mary's death. He might be better another time." I didn't want to lose Rachel now that I found her again.

"Maybe. Right now, I just want to bury those ashes and go back home. Teddy couldn't even accept the comic books we chose for him without retreating into silence."

"Does he know we're trying to find Joseph's killer?"

"The whole town knows."

I listened to my clock cuckoo eight times before I said, "Did you tell him what we found out?"

"Just before you came. It upset him even more."

"Did he know anything? Know if Lucille and Eric were sleeping together then?"

"He said that Joseph shared a lot with him. Joseph knew about Hank's cigarettes and drugs, but he never told Teddy anything about Lucille."

"What about Seth?"

"He said Seth was irrelevant. So was his relationship with Bertha. He didn't use her name, just called her that old lady librarian."

I stood up to clear our coffee mugs and plates. I put them into the dishwasher where we had stacked our dinner dishes, and left the wine glasses on the counter to wash in the morning. Rachel was still sitting and staring out the window when I finished. I stood behind her chair and rubbed her shoulders. We had only tomorrow and Friday before she boarded a plane for New Orleans on Saturday. The cold case wasn't thawing fast enough, and I feared she'd leave more haunted than when she arrived.

She removed my hands and stood up. "Do you have anything I can draw with? Sometimes it relaxes me."

"I'm not an artist. But I have plenty of computer paper and pencils. No colored ones, though."

"I'll do a pencil sketch. Come into the living room. I'll draw you."

Beethoven came back into the kitchen and started crunching his food. "Even better," said Rachel. "I'll draw you holding Beethoven in your lap. Let's carry that rocking chair downstairs. We'll set it in front of the woodstove."

"A study in domesticity?"

"A good title. Something both of us can only imagine."

The rocking chair where I had nursed Cathy now faced the woodstove. Behind me, I could hear pellets of hail hitting the window. They had created a background rhythm to the Dr. Seuss books I used to read to my child. I silently said the words, "BIG C, little c, What begins with C?" the answer morphed from "camel" to "Cathy on the ceiling C... c... C." I wanted to hold her, hear her giggles. Instead, I patted Beethoven, trying to find comfort in his purring. Rachel said nothing as she sketched. I watched her hand moving the pencil. Long strokes, then short, quick ones as she filled in details.

The fire began to die down, and my back screamed that I needed to stretch. Beethoven stretched for me, jumped off my lap, and headed to his litter box in the cellar. I moved forward slightly, then settled back into position. The cuckoo clock cried out ten. It had taken us a long time to gather paper, sharpen pencils, and find a flat surface Rachel could hold in her lap. We settled for a wooden cutting board, arranged the chair with me on it, and situated Rachel so she could include the window behind me in her drawing. I had been patient at first, but now I'd been sitting for over an hour. I wanted to go to bed.

Rachel set down the pencil and wiggled her fingers.

"Finished?" I put my hands on the arms of the rocking chair to push myself up.

"Sit down. Just give me another minute." Rachel sounded almost hostile, like an artist whose moment of inspiration was being interrupted by the mundane.

The minute turned into fifteen before she finished. I stood, leaned my spine backward, then forward to touch my toes, then backward again. Rachel set the cutting board and pencil next to the pencil sharpener on my end-table barrel. She handed me the drawing that she'd labeled, *Woman in Chair with Cat.*

My heart fluttered into my stomach when I looked at the drawing. It showed me with the same hair, bangs flipped back from my forehead, but with glasses on like the oversized ones I'd worn in high school. Instead of a window behind me, Rachel had drawn an image of the top of the barn, the cow's eyes looking down toward me, watching. I choked back a sob at the way she had turned Beethoven into a human baby. My hand trembled as I held the drawing to her. "What have you done?"

"It's yours." She turned to the stairs, leaving me alone with the drawing, wondering if she even realized what she had drawn.

19

I WOKE—AGAIN—TO THE sound of Rachel in the shower I'd had installed in my claw foot tub. I'd soaked for an hour last night after Rachel showed me her drawing, but it didn't help. I was still thinking of it as I rolled from my stomach onto my side and opened my eyes to the window. The trees in Andy's yard next door glistened with ice. Sleet had bulleted the window most of the night. I'd listened to it at midnight, at 1:30, at 2:45. When I woke for the last time to a nightmare cry coming from Rachel's room, my clock read 4:10 and the storm was over.

The cuckoo clock sounded seven, and I heard the coffee grinder scream. Beethoven jumped off my bed as he'd been doing every morning when the coffee turned on. I should get one with a quieter grinder, but I liked what I had.

I forced myself out of bed and put on my robe and slippers. Rachel's drawing lay face down on the top of a low table I kept under the window to hold whatever book I planned to read next. I told myself I'd been mistaken, that the drawing was of forty-seven-year-old me holding Beethoven. Dots of sunlight sparkled on it. Holding my breath, I turned it over. It hadn't changed. The baby was still a baby, I still looked seventeen, and the cow still stared at me. Rachel's art might be disturbing, but it was also good. She'd shaded my hair and half my face and swaddled the baby in a blanket that she'd covered with tiny pencil lines. She'd balanced the blanket with tiny lines of sleet falling on the cow and the window behind me. I remembered her expression when she handed it to me. Like she didn't recognize what she'd drawn, or that she did and it terrified her. I understood why she came to Shelby if images like this had been intruding into her art work for months.

I turned the drawing over and told myself not to think about it. Just as I walked past the bathroom, Rachel opened the door, her long slender body wrapped in a towel like a half-sari, her hair wet and smooth. Was she some kind of Egyptian seer who had known that Mary was going to die? Had that premonition triggered the intrusion into her dreams?

She touched the urn I had picked up before I left my bedroom. "It feels like ice."

"It's cold upstairs. Get dressed and come have coffee. I need to go to work if I'm going to be away from the library all afternoon."

"Can I come with you? I don't want to stay here alone."

"Are you afraid? Whoever left those messages to forget Joseph won't come after us unless we find real evidence."

"We're going to find the killer today." She took her hand off the urn and warmed it on her towel.

"Why do you say that?"

"A premonition. I get them sometimes." Her dark eyes stared into mine. Maybe she *was* a seer. I pushed aside the thought that she wanted to confess something.

The urn safely stored in a cupboard away from Beethoven, we stepped into a world that looked like an ice palace. Sun was hitting ice-covered tree branches empty of leaves.

"Wait." Rachel stopped my hand from locking my door.

"What's wrong?"

"Nothing. I want to get paper and pencil. While you work, I'll find a window at the library and sketch. This is too beautiful not to capture it."

I glanced at the window of my car. "There's no reason to scrape ice off my car. I'll get the urn and a couple of trowels. We won't have to come back for them. We can stop at Nicole's flower shop, and then walk to the cemetery."

"Teddy's bringing trowels, shovels, an ice pick. All you need are the ashes."

"Is he bringing a blowtorch?"

"Yes," she said as we went inside.

When we came outside again, Rachel carried a canvas bag with paper and pencils, and I held the urn in one arm while I locked the door. I put my keys into the pocket of my parka, along with enough money to buy flowers that would die on the grave.

The puddles in my driveway were coated with a skim of ice. We stopped at each one, cracking the ice with our feet. Something about ice shattering like glass drew both kids and adults. It didn't thunder the way ice moving on the lake thundered and made me stop whenever I skated. Shattering puddle ice was quieter. The edges cracked when water seeped through, making designs as fine-lined as the ones Rachel drew with her pencil. We stopped in front of my mailbox and poked through one last ice-skimmed puddle. A shard of ice landed like a knife next to Andy's baseball.

Rachel bent to pick up the ball. "What's this?"

"Leave it. It belongs to Andy Carkin." I wondered why it was still there. He should have found it after I talked with him yesterday.

We walked through ice-coated branches that overhung the streets. They touched each other and made us feel like we were walking through a tunnel of glass. "Remember that year when ice like this stayed on the trees for a whole week?" I said. "It would soften, then freeze again in the night."

"It was the year Joseph died. I went to his grave every day that week and pretended the tree next to his headstone was heaven. Not that I believed in heaven even then, but it felt good to pretend."

We passed no one on our way to the library except Irwin walking Rufus. They were on the opposite side of the street. I waved, relieved that we didn't need to stop to talk.

The ramp at the library was glazed with enough ice that both of us slid backwards when we tried to climb it. So much for handicap access. I set down the urn at the bottom of the ramp and hung onto the railing when I opened the door. Holding her bag, Rachel used the railing to keep herself from sliding. I slid down the ramp on my feet, enjoying the sensation almost as much as I enjoyed cracking ice. I nestled the urn in one arm and balanced myself with the railing as I climbed back up.

Rachel found a place at the end of the shelves that held the encyclopedias. She sat in one of the chairs we used when she had first arrived. The window it faced overlooked the church. "Forget the church, and just draw the tree near this window," I said as I remembered the figure I saw the day of Joseph's funeral.

"Maybe. It's beautiful with the ice on it."

I left her alone and found some rock salt to sprinkle on the ramp. When the library opened, the ice should have softened enough to make it safe for the few patrons who would venture out this slippery morning.

Rachel handed her drawing to me. "No ghosts this time. I'll leave it here. Another gift for you." Her eyes glazed over. I told myself it was from looking at the ice that was shimmering in the sun, that she didn't hear the emphasis she put on the word "gift."

I studied the drawing. It could have served as an illustration for *The Ice Castle*, a Daisy Dreamer children's book that was one of the library's most checked out. Drawing the pencil lines that covered the dark bark of the tree required patience I didn't have. What was magical was the way she'd been able to use pencil to capture sheaths of ice on the branches. They reflected sunlight, though no sun showed on the page.

"It's beautiful." I hugged her and carried the drawing to my cubicle. Only when I laid it face up on my desk did I see that ice on one of the branches looked like the face of a child. The image seemed to follow me as I put on my parka and lifted the urn.

Rachel was waiting at the door, the canvas bag with paper and pencil flung over her shoulder. "No need to carry that," I said. "If we don't come back here, I have plenty more at my house. Your drawing is amazing. I'd never have the patience to make all those tiny lines."

"It's like meditation. I don't think when I'm drawing. My hands take over. They created no baby last night or this morning. Maybe burying the ashes will be enough to wipe out the images."

Rachel was like an Egyptian hieroglyph I couldn't read. Was she so divorced from reality that she hadn't noticed the tiny faces she'd drawn? After we buried Mary's ashes, I'd show her the drawings and confront her. "I heard you call out in the night. Bad dreams again?"

She nodded. "We were burying Joseph. Seth, Hank, Lucille, and Paul the Pole were all standing over us and laughing. Let's not talk about it. I know what triggered it. Where's the flower shop?"

"Just past the fire station in the little house that used to be a yarn store."

"I remember that store. What happened to it?"

"Mabel Hanrahan owned it. She retired and no one wanted to keep it running. There's not a lot of call for yarn when people can buy sweaters at Walmart."

"Who owns the flower shop? Is it any good?"

"Her name's Nicole. She bought the house and turned it into a flower shop about ten years ago. She does a nice job with whatever flowers she gets delivered from Boston. She arranged the ones for Mary's funeral."

"Whatever we buy will die." Rachel muttered "like Joseph and Mary" under her breath.

"I know. But at least the grave will look nice when we leave it."

Rachel waved her arm above her. "We'll cut some branches and scatter them with the flowers. We can call it *Arrangement in Fire and Ice*."

"I get the reference to Frost's poem, but why fire?"

"We'll buy red flowers. Rachel began to recite the poem I remembered her reading at Joseph's funeral.

> *Some say the world will end in fire,*
> *Some say in ice.*
> *From what I've tasted of desire*
> *I hold with those who favor fire.*

I'd never understood why she chose that poem until she told me about having sex with Joseph. She couldn't have known about her pregnancy then, but she knew about desire, and I knew that the whole of our senior year, she felt like her own life had ended with Joseph's.

At Hank's gas station, we crossed the street so we'd be walking under ice-covered trees instead of along the side of the street tarred over for gas tanks and fire engines. Tiny drops of water fell on us from the ice that clung to the branches. I wanted it never to melt. Hank was pulling the gas nozzle out of someone's tank. He waved the nozzle toward us. *Fire and ice*, I thought as I imagined him dousing us in gas and lighting a match.

Nicole's flower shop identified itself with only a sign nailed to the clapboards next to the entrance. No big sign on the street or attached to the maple tree that shaded it in summer. Today, it looked like a country cottage framed by ice.

Inside was warm and smelled of the fresh cut greens Nicole used for her winter flower arrangements. Nicole stood at the long counter and the sink, flowers and greenery spread in front of her. The tie of her apron draped over her ample bottom. She had one of those pear-shaped figures, small chest and waist, large hips that she de-emphasized by wearing black pants and colorful shirts meant to direct the eye away from her lower half.

A cheerful bell announced us. Nicole turned around, holding a pair of shears in hands made powerful from clipping and arranging. Her apron showed a picture of the shop in summer, shaded by the tree and bordered with a profusion of flowers she kept weeded, deadheaded, and heavily fertilized.

She looked at the urn I carried. "That Mary?"

I liked her directness. "It is. We're on our way to the cemetery to bury her ashes next to her son Joseph."

"Never knew Mary had a son until people started talking about a murder." Nicole held out her hand to Rachel. "You must be the person helping Deborah find his killer."

Rachel shook hands with her glove on. "Is there anyone who *doesn't* know why I'm here? The whole town sounds like a Greek chorus."

"It's a small town," said Nicole. "Only reason I heard about it is Seth Thompson cornered me when I left flowers for the memorial service at the church. He was complaining, 'Mary should be left in peace. So should he.' I had no idea why he was so angry until he told me about her son being murdered in his barn."

Rachel grabbed the shears off the table and began opening and closing them. "We think Seth did it."

I took the shears away from her. "Rachel thinks that. We have no idea who killed Joseph. All we want now are some flowers to put on top of Mary's ashes at his grave."

Nicole looked toward the cooler that held the kind of standard flowers she used in winter. Large spider mums, mostly white, purple delphinium, many colors of Gerber daisies, red and yellow roses. "Everything I have will die in an hour outside."

"We'll just get a couple of red roses," I said. "Can you arrange them with some of that holly? The holly will last."

"And the roses will turn black." Nicole made no move toward the cooler.

"It's a gesture," I said. "I'll clean them off the grave tomorrow."

Nicole opened the cooler and took out two roses and a sprig of holly. "I'll add some pine greens and wrap them with a red ribbon." She arranged them with quick and practiced hands.

I set down the urn so I could get money from my pocket. "How much?"

She handed the flowers to Rachel. "I can't charge for flowers I know are going to die."

"Everything dies." Rachel accepted the flowers and walked out the door.

"She okay?" said Nicole.

"Not really. Joseph was her boyfriend in high school. And Mary was like a mother to her."

"We all miss Mary." Nicole turned back to her counter and began clipping the ends of the spider mums she was working with. She pushed the ends into the sink as if pushing away her own sadness.

Outside, Rachel had crossed the street and was walking fast. I ran to catch up with her. "Slow down."

She held the flower arrangement upright in one hand. At Hank's gas station, she stopped. "I'm going inside. Maybe you're right. Seth didn't kill Joseph, Hank did."

"So you're just going to walk in there and accuse him?"

She ignored me and opened the door to the station. I followed her, afraid of what Hank would do if she started making accusations.

Hank looked up from behind the counter that was covered with receipts and invoices and a sampling of cigarettes. "Well, well. What can I do for you girls?"

"*Women*," I corrected.

Rachel held the flowers in front of her like a weapon. "Did Joseph know? Is that why he quit? Or did you fire him?"

Hank pretended ignorance. "Who's Joseph?"

Rachel set the flowers on the counter and leaned across it so she was eye to eye with Hank. "Joseph Wheeler. You remember. The one who worked for you. The one who knew you were selling *illegal* cigarettes and drugs."

Hank straightened as high as his stocky body allowed. "Sorry. Forgot his name. I don't sell drugs, and my cigarettes are all legal."

Rachel leaned farther over the counter. "That's not what he told me. Was he going to report you?"

"Get the hell out of my garage. I didn't kill that boy."

"No one said you did." Was Hank protesting too much? Is that why he, like Lucille, denied something we hadn't accused him of? I pulled Rachel away from the counter and, grabbing the flowers, directed her out the door.

20

NO ROADS WOUND through what was more a Colonial graveyard than a landscaped cemetery. Teddy's truck was parked beside a pine tree at its edge. The ice on the needles had melted, but the bare branches on the oaks and maples scattered among the graves were still coated. I could see why thirty years ago Rachel would have thought it looked like heaven when she talked to the dead Joseph. I imagined her telling him about her pregnancy and her miscarriage. Asking who killed him. And why.

Joseph's grave was at the far end of the cemetery next to the plots that remained empty. My parents would be buried here. So would Bertha Whetmore. And Seth and Hank in the Thompson and Huckabay plots. I often walked through the old portion, reading the inscriptions on the lichen-covered gravestones and imagining the sorrow of those who lost children whose stones labeled them as six months old or two years old or five. Only a few graves held people who had lived to ninety. One identified Moses Orville Corey, age twenty-four, dead in the Civil War, when so many soldiers' remains never made it home. Iron markers pushed into the ground commemorated other men who fought in one of the world wars.

In nice weather, I'd stop at the grave of Patience Cooper Pomeroy, Died March 20, 1840, Age 3 yrs. The stone showed no verse, no carving of a willow or an urn, only the stark mention of the child's age. I'd tell Patience about Cathy and imagine them playing together in a field. At the opposite end of the cemetery, I'd stand at Joseph's grave and apologize for sending him on a search for his German book. When I left, I'd pretend to leave my sorrow and my guilt, as if I had unburdened myself in a confessional.

Rachel and I walked slowly toward the grave where Teddy was kneeling. I thought he was digging until we got closer and I saw his head resting on the gravestone. Above him, a wisp of a cloud floated through the clear sky like a scarf. The ice was beginning to melt as the sun hit the trees, but under them on the rutted path, the puddles held their skim. I wanted to punch my foot through one, but it would be a gesture of anger now, instead of joy.

When he heard the crunch of our footsteps, Teddy put his hands on the gravestone and pushed himself up. The rims of his eyes were red, but there were no tears. His face showed the controlled emotion I'd seen in him when he spoke about Mary at her funeral. "I never come here," he said. "The stone looks so empty."

I liked its simplicity the same way I liked the simplicity of Patience's stone. Just Joseph James Wheeler, and under that, March 10, 1973 – September 15, 1990.

Rachel lay the flowers on the top of the stone. One end of the red ribbon fell into a water-filled indentation as if it were a resting place. "We could have Mary's name carved onto it."

Teddy handed us a trowel. "It doesn't matter. When we're dead, there'll be no one left who remembers her."

"Elizabeth will." I wanted to add that even Patience Pomeroy gave me someone to talk to.

Teddy started pounding at the ground with an ice pick. Only a few inches of dead grass and dirt loosened. He set down the pick and turned on the blowtorch that he'd stuck into a canvas bag with the trowels he'd given us. "I had to stop at Hank's to get propane for this thing. Guy's a creep."

Rachel touched the hand that was holding the torch. "You know he's one of our suspects."

"Forget it, Rachel. Let's just get this done." He turned on the torch, startling a few nuthatches that had been feeding at a seed cone someone had hung from a tree branch. The flame from the torch loosened tiny pellets of dirt and stone that flew into the air.

Rachel and I moved back as Teddy warmed the earth. He turned off the blowtorch and told us to dig. We kneeled on the wet grass and dug out the dirt that he'd thawed. When we could dig no further, Teddy torched again. We repeated this half-a-dozen times—torch, trowel, torch—until we had a hole twelve inches deep. It wasn't exactly round, but its diameter was wide enough to provide a safe place for Mary's ashes. No squirrel would dig them up.

Teddy picked up the urn and placed it in the hole, its earthen color lighter than the deep soil.

"Wait," I said, reaching down for the urn. "Just the ashes. No separation from the earth and Joseph."

Teddy straightened and stepped back from the grave. "There's already a separation. He's in his coffin, remember."

"Deb's right," said Rachel. "We should hold the ashes in our hands before we bury them."

"I'll plant violets in the spring. They'll flourish every year and remind me of Mary when she was alive." I opened the lid and reached my hand in for some ashes. They felt like fireplace ashes, only coarser with some hard bits that I could tell were bone that hadn't fully burned. I dropped them into the hole and passed the urn to Rachel who first smelled the ashes, then took a handful and sprinkled them into the hole. When she gave Teddy the urn, he tipped it over and dumped out the remaining ashes without touching them. I wanted to call him a coward until he threw the urn against Joseph's headstone, and I saw that he was acting from anger or sorrow, not cowardice. Most of the pottery shards fell into the ashes. I swept the few that had scattered onto the grass and a patch of remaining snow into the hole. I used my hand to mingle them with the ashes and felt something metallic. Mary's wedding ring that Pastor Pam had placed in the urn.

Rachel took it and tried to slip it on her finger. When it didn't fit, she touched it to her lips and, laying it among the ashes, began to fill in the hole. Teddy pushed her aside and shoveled. I knelt to rescue the clump of grass we had dug through.

Rachel found a low hanging branch on the maple tree next to the grave. She broke off several twigs, careful not to disturb their coating of ice. She arranged them with the bouquet of flowers that she placed on top of the grass. "Fire and ice," she whispered.

The three of us stood silent in front of our altar to the dead. I closed my eyes and imagined Mary and Joseph, Nathan and Cathy, all holding hands, even though I didn't believe in a heaven where the flesh rose with the soul. I knew that Teddy and Rachel wouldn't pray with me, so I spoke the end of the twenty-third Psalm. "I will dwell in the house of the Lord forever."

"Nice that you believe that," said Teddy. "I have to go. I'll get Rachel at your house in about an hour." He kissed Rachel on the cheek, the first gesture of love instead of tension I'd seen from him. He picked up his tools and walked quickly to his truck, his posture under his gray jacket making him look more than ever like the tin man.

I watched him turn his truck toward town, and wondered why he hadn't offered us a ride before he went wherever he claimed he needed to go.

I plucked two petals off of one of the roses and handed one to Rachel. She accepted it without speaking. Together, we turned our backs on the grave. Ice cracked from a branch above it and fell onto the stone as if it, too, were mourning. I stopped in front of Patience's grave and rested my petal on the thin stone, its red stark against the moss colored lichens. "I talk to her sometimes," I said.

Rachel read the inscription. "Just three years old when she died. Like your daughter. Does it help?"

"Sometimes."

Rachel set her rose petal next to mine so they touched, forming a shape that resembled a heart. "Rest in peace, Patience Cooper Pomeroy."

We left the cemetery and walked slowly to the library. Rachel waited on the sidewalk in front of the former church building where we used to roller skate. I left her and went inside to tell Jody I wouldn't be back to work that day. When I came outside again carrying the canvas bag with paper and pencils, Rachel pointed down the street to Seth's house. He was locking his door. He kicked a fallen branch and started to turn right until he saw us, then he reversed direction, and hurried our way. Even at a distance, I could see the anger in his body. We were in front of the church when he reached us and grabbed my arm. "Where'd you put it?"

"Put what?" I wrenched my arm free.

"The German book." He grabbed my arm again.

On the opposite side of the street, several people stopped to watch our exchange. Seth would do nothing in front of witnesses. "Why do you care?"

"What are you telling people about me?"

Rachel moved between us. "That you killed Joseph."

"You can't prove that." He put his hand on Rachel's shoulder, giving her more a punch than a push, and walked away from us. He turned left toward Hank's and the fire station.

Rachel started walking so quickly, I nearly had to run to keep up. I glanced down the street toward Hank's. Seth was standing in front of a gas pump talking with him. Something between Seth and Hank didn't look right.

We continued walking under ice-coated trees. They began to

feel more threatening than beautiful. I stopped at my mailbox. The only mail I had was *Time* magazine, its cover announcing another article on the opioid crisis. I put it into the bag with the paper and pencils. Beneath the mailbox, the baseball was gone. Andy must have picked it up. Finally, something was going right.

Rachel locked the door the moment we came inside. She checked the front door to be sure it was also locked while I hung my parka, hat in the sleeve, over the woodstove and put my gloves on the hearth to dry. "You might as well take off your jacket. Teddy's apt to be a while."

"You should come with us. I don't like the idea of leaving you alone."

I patted Beethoven, who was sleeping on his chair. "I have my attack cat."

"Seriously, Deb. Seth might come after you."

"He won't. We have no evidence, and if he did anything, you'd have him arrested."

She kept her parka on and stood at the window watching for Teddy. As I loaded the woodstove, the clock cuckooed two.

Rachel paced until I persuaded her to take off her parka and draw until Teddy arrived. He'd get here when he got here. An hour later, she gave me her drawing of the woodstove, our jackets hanging above it like black and white ghosts. The fire she sketched flamed in raging lines, but no image of a child appeared this time.

She reached for her parka and took her phone out of the pocket. "I'm calling him. He should have been here ages ago." She pressed his number, waited until the answering machine clicked on, and left a message.

"Come have some tea, then try again."

"Coffee. Strong and black and loaded with caffeine." She followed me into the kitchen while I filled the coffee machine with dark roast beans and rummaged through my cabinets to find something to eat. Their emptiness was embarrassing. We shouldn't have skipped lunch. I pulled the loaf of bread I'd bought for my breakfast out of the bread box. "Lady fingers?"

"Toast strips with butter, cinnamon, and sugar. Didn't your mother always make us that?"

"She did and she does." I hadn't talked to my parents since I called to say that Mary died. If they'd known that Rachel was coming for the service, they might have flown home for it. I missed them.

While we ate our lady fingers, I told Rachel about my parents' decision to winter in Florida, about their health, and how they held each other up now that they were over eighty. She told me more about her childhood than she'd ever shared. Teddy used to tag along behind her, calling her Rachie, and asking a torrent of questions about why the cow didn't move on the barn's rafter, why they couldn't buy corn in May, why plants sometimes got too much rain and sometimes not enough.

"When Mum died, Teddy was only nine. He stopped following me and stopped asking questions. He begged my father to build a garden for him and planted bean seeds in April. They germinated and then died, just as our mother had. But he learned. When my father was drunk, he'd retreat to the back yard, finding something to do even in winter. He'd repair the fence he built to keep away woodchucks, or shovel snow off his garden plot so the soil would warm faster. I used to tease him. Snow was nature's fertilizer. It kept the ground insulated. By the time he was twelve, he figured that out and found indoor sports to keep him busy when he couldn't be outside in the garden or playing baseball."

"I remember your father coaching us in Little League. Teddy was the youngest on the team and one of the best players."

"It was hard for him when my father decided he loved booze more than coaching."

"I wonder why Teddy stopped playing in high school."

"He told me the team felt too empty without Joseph. He had as hard a time that year as I did."

I glanced at my watch. "Maybe you should try calling again. It's almost four o'clock."

She picked up her phone that had sat silent on the kitchen table and tried again. "Teddy, where are you? I'm getting worried."

"Try Janet," I said. "Maybe she knows where he is."

She pressed Janet's number. I heard only Rachel's part of the conversation.

"He didn't come home?

"We're worried, too.

"I'll have Deb take me back.

"It'll be okay. We'll leave a note on the door."

She hung up. "Janet's worried. Said Teddy was tied in knots thinking about burying Mary's ashes. He wouldn't let her come with him. I'm afraid he knows Seth killed Joseph and has gone after him."

"We don't know who killed Joseph. How could Teddy know that?"

"Maybe putting together what I've told him with something he remembers. Take me to his house now and stay there with me."

"I'll wait until Teddy gets home, then decide if I should stay with you."

Rachel went into the living room for our coats while I found a sticky note and wrote, "We went to your house. We'll see you there." No question about where have you been. Wherever he'd gone, I didn't think he knew who killed Joseph. I didn't want to think that he could have been the teenage killer. I wrote no accusation. Just a simple note whose sticky edge I reinforced on the door with a piece of tape.

I already needed headlights when we got into the car. It was just after four o'clock and the sky was turning to dusk. There'd be a huge

Wolf Moon, and a myriad of stars would appear in the still, clear sky. The dampness had gone from the air, and the ice on the trees would sparkle under the moonlight.

We drove past Lucille's house where an extra car in her driveway told me the biology teacher was visiting again. As we came into the center of town, I glanced down the side street toward Hank's garage. It was fully lit and open for service. Or cigarettes. Seth's house was dark. I clutched the steering wheel tighter, wondering why he wasn't home. A group of teenagers were going into The Village Store, book bags flung over their shoulders. The church's front light had come on as if to welcome people even though the doors would be locked. Jody was locking the library door. The town was folding up for its usual quiet January night.

My car wheels skidded on a piece of black ice when I took the turn at Teddy's farm stand.

"Careful," said Rachel.

"It'll be okay now. There won't be ice on the dirt."

The sun was almost fully set when we reached the barn. Just under the watchful eyes of the cow, we saw Teddy's truck. I pulled behind it and stopped the car. We got out and held onto each other as we walked toward the barn. Behind us something shot across the road, the first of the nocturnal animals, a premonition invading me. We joined our hands to grab the barn door and slide it open.

21

WE LEFT THE barn door open to the rising shape of the full moon. Teddy sat, barely visible, on the tractor. He must have heard us, but he didn't turn. He kept tossing something from hand to hand. He stopped only when I tripped over the canvas bag that held the tools he'd brought to the cemetery.

Rachel stood in front of one of the tractor's tires and called to him as if he were on an enormous front loader instead of a tractor for a tiny farm. Her voice echoed through the barn. "Get down, Teddy. We need to go home."

He stopped tossing whatever was in his hand. "Too many memories." He turned on the seat and jumped, landing with his knees bent in a move that he must have practiced in his years of farming. In front of the tractor, he sat on the hay bale and began tossing what I could see was a baseball that gave my premonition a shape.

Rachel nudged him to the edge of the bale and sat beside him, laying her head on his shoulder. I bent to stop his tossing, pretending I hadn't connected the ball to Joseph's death. "Andy Carkin dropped a baseball near my mailbox."

Still holding the ball, he said something I couldn't hear. Rachel heard and moved out of his arm, turning to look at him. "That was yours? Why was it at Deb's?"

Teddy spoke louder now. "I threw it at her mailbox. The night of the rain storm."

"Why would you do that?" I wanted to give him an excuse, give myself time to get Rachel out of the barn.

He began digging in the frozen dirt with his foot. "You need to back off. Joseph's dead. Let him stay that way."

I stepped in front of the hay bale, close enough that I could lunge at Teddy and give Rachel time to run. "Did you leave those warnings? And the telephone message? And the message in the snow on my car?"

Teddy stopped his futile digging and tossed the ball again. "I did. And I threw that sketch of Joseph into the manure hole. You invaded the one place I come to find some peace. Back off, okay?"

Rachel put her hand on his thigh. She drew him closer to her. "It's done. I've had enough of it. Seth Thompson murdered Joseph. We'll never prove it, but that's okay. At least we know what happened."

Teddy shoved Rachel and jumped to his feet, dropping the ball onto the hay strewn in front of the bale. He kicked the hay around it and spit out, "You're fucking wrong!"

Rachel sat immobile on the bale. I stood inches in front of Teddy and forced him to look at me when I said, "*You* killed him."

He spun around and shoved me down next to Rachel. He towered over us. I could hear his breathing getting heavier. It stopped before he spoke in a whisper. As quiet as his voice was, it filled the barn. "Now you know I killed my best friend."

The barn erupted with Rachel's fury. She leaped to her feet and began pounding her brother, sobbing and screaming. "I hate you! I hate you!"

I jumped up, trying to pull her away while unleashing my own fury. "Bastard. How *could* you? He was your friend."

Rachel flailed between Teddy and me. Her fist landed on my stomach, knocking me backwards. I doubled over, my gut clenching.

I righted myself and started to run for the door, pulling Rachel along with me. She was still screaming, "I hate you," as if her hate could undo the past.

Teddy was too fast. He caught us beside the tractor, wrapping an arm around each of us. He knocked over one of the gas cans as he dragged us through the sawdust next to his power saw. My sleeve caught on the edge and tore. He pushed us onto the hay bale and I reached into my pocket for my phone. He knocked it away. It hit the tractor with a metallic clang. His anger ebbed to a quiet plea. "I'm not going to hurt you. One death's enough. Just let me explain."

I held Rachel to me. She had lost Elizabeth's hat, and her hair fell wild against my shoulder. Sobs shook through her body. She tried to stand up, but Teddy pushed her down again, less violently this time. He wasn't going to kill us. It was over. I hugged Rachel harder and whispered, "Shh. Breathe."

Teddy began rocking from foot to foot, his tall body only a shadow in the dim moonlight coming through the barn door. I knew then that his was the shadow I saw outside the church window the day of Joseph's funeral. Joseph was his friend. Teddy had been carrying thirty years of guilt. From the depths of my own pain, I tried to imagine his. After the sharpness of the first year, a steady, droning, gnawing sense of guilt.

Rachel dug her fingers into my waist. I could feel the fury and fear that was even stronger than mine. We were two women holding each other as tight as we could.

Teddy stood over us like a preacher, like Charles Tibbetts trying to explain the unexplainable. "It was an accident. I followed Joseph to the barn and sat outside long enough to chug three of the beers we were supposed to take to Eric's. I don't know why Joseph rode his bike to the barn. Still don't. But I wanted him to leave Rachel alone. I needed her."

He stooped and touched Rachel gently on the face. "Dad was drunk every single day then. I couldn't lose you to Joseph."

She jerked her face away. "So you acted like Dad. You're worse than he ever was!"

He straightened. "You're right. I was as drunk as Dad when I finished those beers. When I went into the barn, Joseph was looking for something in one of the stalls. I got close and screamed at him to leave you alone. I wrestled him out of the stall, but he didn't want to fight. He just stood behind an empty wheelbarrow like it was some kind of shield. He started to leave. The last thing he said to me was 'I love her.' Then I pulled this out of my pocket."

Teddy stooped to the hay to pick up the baseball he began tossing again. It looked like a pendulum ticking away thirty years of secrecy darker than the barn in the seeping moonlight. "We were playing catch earlier. I wish I had put the ball back in my room, but Dad was drunk. I watched you go upstairs to bed and then go out again."

His voice became manic. "Joseph was heading out of the barn when I threw the ball as hard as I could. It hit him on the side of the head, and then fell just outside the door. I didn't know he was dead. I picked up the ball, closed the door, and left. I didn't even hear him fall. When you found him, it was too late to explain what had happened."

I loosened my grasp on Rachel. "It *wasn't* too late. You could have explained. You didn't intend to kill him."

"I've been telling myself for thirty years that I didn't mean to hit him. But I know I did. Drunk as I was, I could still hit my target." Teddy cocked his arm. I ducked, pulling Rachel down with me when he turned and threw the baseball. It hit the back wall of the barn, echoing into the rafters.

I reached toward Teddy and touched his arm. "You've spent thirty years carrying around the guilt of killing your friend. You should have just gone to the police."

He recoiled. "I was afraid. So instead, I moved on, built a life. You broke my peace. Now get the hell out before I do something else I'll regret."

I helped Rachel stand and, walking past the tractor, picked up my phone. We held our gloved hands together when we closed the barn door. A fisher cat crossed in front of Teddy's truck. We could hear Teddy inside throwing his baseball against the wall and cursing. The sound stopped as we reached my car. We leaned against it, and I peeled off my gloves to swipe my phone. Rachel stopped me. "Don't call the police."

"We have to tell them."

"I have to think. He's my brother."

She tried to grab my phone. I held it and backed away to the driver's side of the car. We stood there, the car a barrier between us as strong as the thousand miles that had kept us separated all these years. Under the moon and stars, I could see her shivering even as she lay her forehead on the cold window. I waited. Maybe she was right. Maybe we should let Teddy's guilt be enough punishment. More pain wouldn't change the past.

I looked up at the loft window. The cow's head shone through what I thought was a halo of fog despite the clear evening. Slowly the halo deepened. The gas cans. The sawdust. The blowtorch. I knew what Teddy had done.

Rachel ran toward the door. I pressed 911 and screamed out our location as I ran to her. Together, we pushed on the handle. The door opened to a landscape of smoke, its acrid smell choking us. I unzipped my parka and pulled it in front of my face. Beneath the roar of the flames, I could hear Teddy screaming in front of the tractor that had started to burn. We found a path on the opposite side of the table saw in time to see a funnel of flame collapse on the burning hay bale. The screaming stopped. The flames that had already engulfed the loft ignited a rafter that exploded in front of Rachel. The fire jumped into the stalls, roaring as if cows were caught in the flames.

Coughing, my eyes burning, I dragged Rachel by the waist toward the open door. The outside air fed the fire until the whole barn was engulfed. I kept dragging her until we were at the edge of the road, safe from the flames. We collapsed on the ground, Rachel sobbing in my arms and chanting, "He's my brother. He's my brother."

I watched as the flames burned through the cow's head and its remains fell to the ground.

I sat in the back pew waiting for Rachel, who asked me to meet her in the sanctuary after the Sunday service. She wanted to say goodbye. "No Pastor Pam. I'm done with ministers," she said in the brief moment she spoke to me at Teddy's funeral. She'd avoided me during the days of mourning, and I'd left her to decide if she would call the police. I knew now that she'd hold Teddy's secret the way she had held her pregnancy secret.

During all those years we were separated, Rachel hadn't forgiven herself. She'd harbored her secrets and her sorrow while I found a way to move forward. I wanted her to find closure, to find a path the way I had. Church comforted me. It had taken me a long time after Cathy and Nathan to embrace it. Teddy's death brought me closer than ever to this sanctuary. The early morning sun shone now through the stained-glass windows, dappling my hands with light.

Our little church had been filled to overflowing for Teddy's funeral. Lucille spoke about Teddy as a high school student and as a farmer. Listening to her, I still couldn't decide if she had slept with a teenager. Seth and Hank had come to the funeral, perhaps to show Rachel and me that they weren't guilty. They didn't know that we'd solved the murder, that the details had burned up with the barn.

When the police and fire chief talked with Rachel and me, we said that Teddy had gone there after we buried Mary's ashes. He often went to the barn to remember Joseph, who had been his best friend. None of them remembered the case. Even though they wouldd continue their investigation, I knew they accepted that the fire was an accident, a careless handling of a blowtorch too near gas and sawdust and hay.

The front door to the church opened. I twisted in the pew and watched Rachel enter the sanctuary. The multi-colored scarf she wore draped over her tunic length sweater relieved its black. She looked more than ever like Cleopatra.

She slid in next to me, holding herself stiff and facing the front of the church as she spoke. "Please don't tell anyone. Teddy's my brother. Let him rest in peace."

I thought of the cow in the rafters and how every time I passed the barn I imagined the eyes of Dr. T. J. Eckleburg looking down on me and judging. Its burning hadn't burned away my guilt. "If I hadn't left the German book…"

"If I hadn't made Teddy feel like I abandoned him…"

"If Teddy hadn't been drunk…"

"We're all guilty," I said.

Rachel raised her hand to her hair then returned it to her lap. "I wanted to say goodbye here. I don't understand it, but I know this church brings you comfort."

"I wish you could find a place to comfort you."

"I have my studio. I'll be okay now that we know what happened. I won't be coming back."

I thought of Janet who was mourning her husband the way I had mourned Nathan. Elizabeth would bring her comfort, but Elizabeth would have no father. Maybe it would be better for her than having a drunk father had been for Teddy and Rachel. "What about Janet and Elizabeth?"

"Elizabeth wants me to come back. She's started making a new hat to replace the one that burned up with the barn and Te—" She choked back the name. "It hurts too much to be here. Teddy killed the boy I love."

"Loved," I said. "You need to move on."

"Janet knows."

"Knows that Teddy lit that blowtorch on purpose?"

"Not that. I let her think it was an accident."

"Maybe it was." I wanted to find a way to give Rachel comfort.

"No. You know better. Janet knows how Joseph died. Teddy told her before they were married. She loved him anyway."

"She helped him accept his guilt."

"Like I said, she loved him. She's in her car waiting for me." Rachel slid out of the pew without touching me. I stood and watched her leave, her posture, the same rigid tin as her brother.

I walked to the front of the sanctuary and climbed the steps to the pulpit. A Bible rested on it. I opened to Luke 17: 3, a passage I remembered Reverend Tibbetts often quoting to our youth group when one of us was angry with another. "If thy brother trespass against thee, rebuke him; and if he repent, forgive him."

The words of the Bible followed me as I left the church. I thought of the German book, and of Nathan and Cathy and how I had let them drive away for ice cream. It was easier to forgive Teddy than to forgive myself.

The church bell tolling noon rang when I stepped outside into sunlight that was warming the crisp air. Across the street, Irwin Trombly was walking Rufus. Maybe some day. For now, I waved and walked on home alone.

ACKNOWLEDGMENTS

IN A SMALL town in Massachusetts, a barn with a wooden cow's head peeking out from the rafters sits close to the road. When I was a child, I thought the cow was real. When I was a young mother, my daughter also thought it was real. Returning to Massachusetts for a visit a few years ago, I saw it again, still watching over whoever passed. Thus was born the first scene of *The Barn*.

Grateful acknowledgment to whoever owns this barn and keeps it, unlike my imagined one, in pristine condition. Thank you, as well, to Nancy Dole, who grew up on a dairy farm and saved me from mistakes involving stalls and stanchions. I am, as always, indebted to my Monday Mayhem writers group. The late Tim Wolforth (Jim Wolf Mysteries) founded the group and kindly allowed me to join when I moved to Oregon. Jenn Ashton (first novel in progress), Carole Beers (Pepper Kane Mysteries), Michael Niemann (Valentin Vermeulen thrillers), and Clive Rosengren (Eddie Collins Mysteries) provide invaluable feedback twice each month. Larry Maness (Jake Eaton Mysteries) and Alan Thompson (*The Peninsula)* read a full draft of *The Barn* and offered helpful suggestions. Special thanks to Cynthia Brackett-Vincent and Eddie Vincent, who have welcomed me to Encircle Publications for this first Deborah Strong mystery.

As always, I thank my husband, Ron Dean, for reading drafts

and being my most vocal champion. Our daughter, Emily Warren, massaged out my computer neck cramps, and our son, Michael Dean, has moved around the world to settings I can use for another Deborah Strong Mystery. To my grandchildren Juliana, Ryan, and Jasper, thank you for growing into avid readers. The next book will be dedicated to you.

ABOUT THE AUTHOR

Sharon Dean grew up in Chelmsford, Massachusetts, where she and her two siblings rode bikes, read books, and visited the historical sites made famous by the Pilgrims, the Revolutionaries, and the many famous writers of New England's nineteenth century. From Massachusetts, it was a small leap to the University of New Hampshire and a degree in English.

When she returned to Chelmsford after graduation, Sharon discovered that she shouldn't teach seventh graders and that she should marry the man she dated in college. They spent a year in Del Rio, Texas, where she had a more successful year of teaching high school while her husband completed Air Force pilot training. When he was assigned to Pease Air Force Base in New Hampshire, she seized the opportunity to enter graduate school at UNH.

Armed with a Ph.D. and facing a declining job market, Sharon spent several years laboring on the adjunct teaching circuit before she began a full-time career at Rivier University in Nashua, New Hampshire. She added the aura of the nineteenth century to her life when she and her husband purchased an 1865 farmhouse in nearby Brookline. Four academic books later, Sharon has become professor emerita and has moved with, yes, the same husband to Ashland, Oregon, where her daughter is raising a child of the West, and her son has established an American base while he raises his children as ex-pats, currently in The Hague. Embracing a change she never anticipated, Sharon is learning to bike and hike and garden in the Siskiyous instead of the White Mountains. She has sworn off books that require footnotes, and is reinventing herself as a writer of mystery novels.